My Life With Penny

My Life With Penny

Marianne Mjelva

Translated by Osa K. Bondhus

Copyright: © Marianne Mjelva 2009
Original title: Livet med Penny
Cover and inside illustrations © 2009 Ketil Jakobsen Productions AS
Cover layout: © Stabenfeldt AS
Translated by Osa K. Bondhus

Typeset by Roberta L. Melzl
Editor: Bobbie Chase
Printed in Germany, 2009

ISBN: 978-1-934983-09-6

Stabenfeldt, Inc.
225 Park Avenue South
New York, NY 10003
www.pony4kids.com

Available exclusively through PONY.

Chapter 1

"How are we going to live through this?" I muttered into the mane of my little black pony. I let out a loud, exaggerated sigh, which made my mom roll her eyes. I was going on a vacation with my family, for *two whole weeks* in Spain. And I was upset because I had to be away from my beautiful pony that long.

"Oh, come on, Julia! It's only a couple of weeks, and you'll even get to ride while you're in Spain! Penny will be perfectly fine here. She'll be taking it easy and enjoying the summer pasture. And when you get back, she'll be all rarin' to go!"

"Yeah, yeah," I answered. "It's just that I'll miss her so much!"

"Don't worry about Penny, Julia. She'll love the large summer pasture in the woods, and either Anette or I will go up there every day to check on her and make sure she gets her minerals and garlic. There's also plenty of fresh water in the creek that runs right through the pasture. Come on, don't you want to take her outside before you leave?"

These sensible words, which by the way I had heard before, came from my loyal friend and riding instructor,

Linn Iversen, who was also the owner of the stable where I boarded Penny. I nodded and started walking. Linn followed me to the gate, and when I gave Penny a kiss on the muzzle and pulled off her halter, leaving her free to run off, Linn said, "I bet she won't even miss you!"

As if *that* was going to make me feel better! I watched Penny as she ran off toward her best friend, Prisci. The two of them ran side by side across the grassy meadow and into the woods until they reached the fence at the other end. Then they stopped, turned around, and came storming back to us again, stopping short right in front of the gate. Penny let out a loud and happy neigh, and I gave her one last hug before I left her and went back down to Mom, who was waiting in the car.

"Finally, we're on our way!" We were on the plane, and Mom sank into her seat next to Dad, then turned and smiled to Cecilie and me, as we were across the aisle from them.

"Oh, goodie! We're *finally* leaving Norway– just the wonderful country where my horse happens to be– just so we can lie flat on a beach, frying to a crisp among a million other tourists," I said sarcastically. I was still a little grumpy about having to leave my pony for two weeks.

"Give it a rest, will you?" Cecilie pushed a sharp elbow into my arm. "I happen to be looking forward to a few days of lounging lazily on a beach, going swimming and getting a nice tan. So don't try to destroy my good mood with your negativity!"

I rubbed my arm and was tempted to push back, but since Cecilie, who had just turned 16, was two years older than I am, I figured it wasn't such a good idea.

Instead, I dove into my backpack, which I had as a carry-on, and fished out a bunch of pictures from the riding center that I had brought with me. I laid them out on the little fold-down table in front of me and uttered a sigh of self-pity as I studied them.

One of the pictures, of Penny and her horse friends in the paddock, caught my eye. I could easily picture them, the six ponies who at the moment were together in the summer pasture, and who had known each other for a long time. There were the two geldings, Pontus and Baldrian, who were both Welsh Cobs – one black and the other one brown. Then there was Cilla, a red New Forest mare who used to be very nervous. Her owner, who had had her for three years now, had done a lot of work with her and now she was a sweet and trusting pony. Conny was a beautiful dapple Connemara pony, and Prisci, Penny's best friend, was a dark gray dapple Welsh Mountain mare. The photo of Prisci, which showed her looking straight at me with pointed ears, reminded me of how I got to know her and her owner, Pia...

It was just an ordinary day at the end of March last year. I was in the stable, unsaddling Penny after a short and unpleasant ride in the woods (it had rained cats and dogs the entire time, hence we were soaked and miserable).

Suddenly I heard the sound of a powerful engine outside, not that that was such an unusual thing, because most of the people who ride at Linn's stable arrive by car. But when someone yelled, "Here they are!" and at least five of the people who were in the stable ran outside into the rain, I couldn't help but wonder what was going on, so I joined them. A huge horse trailer was parked in the farmyard and was still idling. It made a lot of noise and spewed exhaust, and the driver eventually realized that he needed to turn it off before unloading.

"What's going on here? Are we getting some new horses at the stable?" I asked curiously, nudging Camilla lightly. She was Cilla's owner.

"Yes! Haven't you heard? Linn told us yesterday," said Camilla excitedly. I was about to tell her that I have a guy who exercises Penny on Wednesdays, but before I had a chance to say anything, she continued.

"A celebrity horse is moving in!" Camilla giggled, then rambled on. "It's a retired champion racehorse that's coming here to stay for the remainder of his life! His new owner is going to train him to be a regular riding horse, because apparently he's been racing – until a few weeks ago – and he's very temperamental."

"Do you mean a genuine Thoroughbred stallion?" I asked, impressed, while Camilla just nodded. She was focusing on the driver who was unlocking the trailer. Then I spotted a lady I had never seen before. She looked like she might be in her 40s, with short, blonde hair and broad shoulders. She was tall, and looked strong and determined, so I guessed if anyone was going to turn a temperamental racing stallion into a sensible riding horse, it would be this woman!

Linn and several of the other horse owners at the stable, including a young girl I hadn't seen before, now stood waiting around the horse trailer.

Finally the ramp was lowered, and the driver started unloading a big, chestnut Thoroughbred stallion. Even though it was raining and he was more or less hidden by a waterproof transport cover, he was the perfect picture of a racehorse, with well-trained muscles, sound health and spirit. But there was also a suggestion of something wild and unreachable in his eyes, as if he had never bonded with anything or anybody in his life. The lady with the determined look on her face took the lead rope and started walking the stallion around the farmyard, allowing him to calm down and stretch his legs.

"This guy could probably do with a two hour gallop! We spent an hour trying to get him into the trailer, and his groom said he hadn't had any exercise before he left," said the driver before he went back into the trailer. I was puzzled. Were there more horses arriving? Then my attention was drawn toward the stallion again. He was clearly upset; he reared, flapped his ears and neighed loudly. Unfortunately nobody answered him, because all the other horses were either inside the stable or busy training in the indoor arena because the weather was so bad. This made things worse, because the stallion laid his ears flat, and started stepping around in circles to make it plain as day how annoyed he was.

Linn exchanged a few words with the new lady, and reluctantly the horse followed his new owner as she led him into one of the stable buildings at the ranch, Stable A, where the big horses are kept.

When I turned to the horse trailer again, a young girl whom I hadn't seen before stood on the ramp and took a lead rope handed to her by the driver. At the end of the rope was the prettiest Welsh Mountain pony I'd ever seen! Well, except for Penny, of course! It was a beautiful, gray dapple mare, who obediently and excitedly walked down the ramp. Linn went over to the girl and together they took the pony to Stable B, where all the ponies live. The driver pushed the ramp back in place, and as there was clearly nothing more to see, I ran back into the stable to finish taking care of Penny.

Over the next week, I got to know more about the newcomers at Linn's Stable: The pretty little Welsh Mountain mare named Priscilla, her owner Pia, and the new Thoroughbred stallion named Fireproof Chestnut. The owner of Fireproof Chestnut, Eline Sandersen, was a completely anti-social person who didn't talk to anybody except Linn. She would come in, do her chores, train her horse and leave again.

Pia, on the other hand, was older than I had first thought, but she was so short and thin that you'd think she was only ten. However, she was almost twelve at the time, which made her only a year younger than I am. We hit it off instantly, because Pia was, and still is (!), outgoing, full of life, fun to be with, and a very good rider for someone her age. Her delicate build made her perfectly suited for Priscilla, and she would likely be able to ride her pony for several more years if she didn't grow too much.

Pia, Priscilla, Penny and I started going for trail rides together several times a week, and our two mares bonded and became very attached to each other. At the same time, Pia and I also got to know each other better. Soon we were best friends and started hanging out away from the stable as well.

"I've been thinking," Pia started saying one day when we were mucking out the stalls.

"Really? Congratulations!" I said teasingly, and the next second I was ducking to avoid a handful of sawdust that Pia had thrown at me.

"No, seriously! I've decided that Priscilla is too long a name for everyday use," she continued.

"Oh, yes, it's really long and difficult!" I went on teasingly. Pia scowled, and then raised a hayfork full of horse dung with a threatening look at me. I laughed and waved my arms to ward her off.

"Anyway, since 'Cilla' is already taken, I've decided to call her Prisci! What do you think?" Pia raised her eyebrows, looking questioningly at me. I tried out the name a few times.

"Prisci... Prisci... Yeah, it's cute, it suits her," I said. Pia smiled happily and continued with the mucking. As usual it didn't take long before she started chatting again...

"When is Penny due for new shoes? Prisci is getting new shoes on –" she started saying, but was interrupted.

"Who's Prixie? Is there another new horse around here? That's a lot of new arrivals in just three weeks!"

The comment came from Lisa, the owner of Pontus, a black gelding. She had just walked in the door so Pia explained to her about Priscilla's new nickname.

"I see. Good idea! Maybe I should call Pontus something shorter too?" she pondered.

"Nah, I don't think so. Pontus is already pretty short and simple. I wonder if..." Lisa rambled on. Pia and I exchanged knowing looks as we giggled quietly. Lisa was the chattiest person either of us had *ever* known. She was worse than Pia and I put together!

"Have you heard how things are going with the new stallion?" she asked as she grabbed a wheelbarrow and hayfork and went into Pontus's stall to muck out.

"Yeah, apparently it's going very well! One thing I'll say for Eline, she really knows her stuff when it comes to horses and horse training!" said Pia enthusiastically.

"That's right," I added. "Chestnut has calmed down considerably since he came here. I think this is a much quieter and less stressful life than the racing environment, and he's got an owner who's extremely dedicated to working with him." Pia and Lisa nodded.

"When I saw them in the indoor arena yesterday, they were riding a great dressage program, doing walking and trotting, and he didn't change gaits or try any other nonsense, even though Conny was being trained at the same time," Lisa told us.

"That sounds great," said Pia with a smile. "I guess things will work out just fine for that crazy horse and his owner!"

✳ ✳ ✳ ✳

I put down a picture of Chestnut standing in the farmyard, looking proud and beautiful, and gave another heavy sigh. Mom looked at me sympathetically, but Cecilie wasn't as understanding.

"Julia, will you quit being so childish? You're going to a gorgeous, sandy beach, crammed with all kinds of good-looking boys for two weeks! How bad could things be?"

I had to smile at the thought of that, and with a slightly more contented feeling I leaned back in my seat.

"And don't forget, you'll get to do some riding too!" added Mom, who obviously wanted me to cheer up.

"I know. I'm sure it'll be a great vacation," I said, trying to sound convincing. "I'm just afraid that I might miss Penny too much!" I added with another sigh, mostly to myself.

"I can't wait to see the resort. It looked so cute in the brochure!" exclaimed Cecilie. Mom nodded, looking delighted. The two of them continued to talk about things we were going to do in Spain and how much fun it would be. I grabbed a random picture from the pile and looked at it, and Cecilie and Mom's voices became a dull background noise. The photo I had picked up showed a Thoroughbred mare named Redrose with her owner, Michelle, sitting on her back. A rosette dangled from the horse's bridle and they both looked very happy. I gave a start at the sudden thought of what had almost happened to that mare only two months ago.

Chapter 2

It was early in the morning on the 1st of May, which is
Labor Day in my native Norway, and the weather was
beautiful. Pia and I had planned to go on a nice, long
ride with our ponies. The day before, we had agreed to
meet at the stable at eight o'clock, but it was eight thirty
already, and still no sign of Pia. I had already taken
Penny outside, and she stood by the long, solid tethering
post in the farmyard, looking around impatiently. In
order to make sure she had plenty of energy for the day's
long ride, I had deliberately avoided riding her very hard
the day before. I kept myself busy brushing her while
waiting for Pia, and wondered why she wasn't there yet.
Then suddenly I heard hoofbeats inside Stable A. *Who
could that be?* I thought. I hadn't seen anyone except
Anette that morning. (For your information: Anette is the
lady who feeds and turns the horses in and out morning
and night.)

Penny and I turned around simultaneously, and then
my mouth fell open in surprise, because right there,
emerging from the stable, his head high and with high
leg lifts, was none other than Fireproof Chestnut! He had

14

no tack on, not even a halter, and he was headed right toward the driveway which leads through an avenue of trees straight down to a major highway! For a moment I was frozen in panic, but then I sprang into action, forcing myself to keep a cool head. For the first time I was annoyed that everything was so tidy and organized at Linn's Stable. Not a single halter or lead rope was lying around anywhere, so there was nothing I could grab quickly to use in catching the horse. I thought fast on my feet and made a brief plan. Calmly, I grabbed a couple of carrot pieces from my pocket, ran to the middle of the driveway and stood in front of Chestnut. I started talking soothingly, holding out my hand with the treats in front of me, and looking down at the ground. The stallion slowed down, looking at me curiously, and came to get the treats. I gave a sigh of relief, patted him, and then took a firm hold of his bangs. He resisted at first. He probably didn't like having some little person he didn't know coming and taking him away! I talked sternly to him, pulling on his bangs, and he actually allowed me to lead him toward Stable A again. But then guess what happened? Just as the stallion and I were about to go inside, more horses came out!

Chestnut instantly reared up and I threw myself aside as he turned and took a couple of running steps away from the stable. There he stopped, turned toward the stable with his head high, nostrils wide open and his ears so pointed that they almost met at the top. The horses who had just appeared in the doorway were: a dapple jumping mare named Firefly, a smaller, roan gelding

named Gollum, Coliseum, the biggest horse in the whole stable, measuring 71 inches to the top of his mane, and a few more of their stable mates. And they were all heading outside!

You can just imagine what a situation I was in! Picture this: Penny was standing by the tethering post staring at them all, neighing curiously and starting to pull at the lead rope she was tied up with. Chestnut didn't seem to know what leg to put down, so he was practically tap dancing as he stood there, keeping a steady eye on Firefly. Coliseum, who's a gigantic dapple Holsteiner gelding, walked unperturbed over to the lawn next to the arena and started grazing, while Gollum trotted toward Penny and started checking her out. *And none of these horses had even so much as a halter on!*

Now you may think that I came up with some super smart idea of what to do about this, but that's not what happened at all! The whole situation was so outrageous and happened so unexpectedly that it was like a comedy routine. I couldn't help myself; I started laughing so hard I had to sit down.

After a couple of minutes I finally came to my senses. When I heard barking inside the stable, and then saw Redrose, a medium big, bay Thoroughbred mare running out of the stable, there was nothing funny about the situation anymore. I ran into the stable, which was pretty much in a state of chaos. The doors to the stalls of the five horses that were now outside stood wide open and Anette's halfblood dapple was roaming around in the hall, sniffing around in search of leftover feed. I knew she was

17

a nice, easygoing mare, so I grabbed hold of her mane and pulled her back into her stall. Then I spotted the source of the chaos, and the reason why the horses had gotten out: Rajsaj, Anette's golden retriever, who usually gets to come with her to work, was standing outside the stall of one of Linn's dressage horses, fiddling with the lock. I ran over and grabbed him by the collar, made sure the lock was properly fastened, and pulled him out of the stable. On my way out I also grabbed three halters and five lead ropes, and then I tied Rajsaj to the tethering post. Next I started calling to the horses, just to discover another problem – a big one!

Chestnut was clearly about to mount Redrose, and I remembered that Redrose was in heat at the moment, and was not supposed to be in contact with *any* stallion, not even a gelding! So I acted spontaneously and with no regard for potential personal risk. Storming toward them, I hollered and waved frantically with the lead ropes I still held in my hands. Fortunately the two lovebirds had not yet started anything, and both of them were generally very friendly toward humans. Chestnut stepped aside nicely as he looked at me, confused. Then he, Redrose, and Penny all started neighing, while Rajsaj barked and I shouted. Thinking back I don't understand why the whole neighborhood didn't come running at the sound of all that ruckus, but I guess that's because the closest neighbor is on the other side of the pastures, pretty far away.

Quickly, I put a halter on Chestnut and practically pulled him toward Stable A. I pushed him into the closest stall, locked it and silently thanked Eline for having trained him so well. Then I hurried back out to the farmyard.

Fortunately, by now, Anette had come out of Stable B to see what was going on outside, and with only one questioning glance at me, she picked up the two halters I had dropped and grabbed hold of Gollum and Firefly. I took over with the mare.

"Go ahead and put her outside. She was fed first, so she's eaten already!" shouted Anette as she ran toward a small paddock with Gollum, opened the gate and led him inside. I let Firefly into another paddock, and after that started chasing after Coliseum...

We were totally focused on catching the Holsteiner, who kept slipping away from us. So when Anette finally got hold of his bangs and led him to his paddock, she gave a sigh of relief and said, "Phew! We did it! That's all of them, I think! But what on Earth happened here?"

That's when I realized I hadn't seen Redrose for a while...

"Um, sorry, but I think Redrose may have taken off," I said timidly. Then I sank down on one of the benches outside the stable.

"What?! Did *she* escape too? And exactly how did all these horses get out of the stable? You didn't let them out, did you?" I preferred to think that this last question was a result of hysteria. I certainly hoped that Anette knew that I never, not even in my sleep, would dream of letting a bunch of horses out of the stable, with great risk to their lives!

"And why is Rajsaj *tied up*, to the *tethering post*?!" she finally burst out angrily.

I could tell that Anette was on the verge of losing it,

but I didn't think she had a good reason to take it out on me! It was, as a matter of fact, *her* dog who had caused the havoc, and if I hadn't just happened to be there that early, it may very well have ended a lot worse! I told her as much, in an icy, high-pitched voice. When I was done, I glared at her for a few seconds and then walked resolutely over to Penny, who had calmed down considerably by now. After a couple of minutes Anette came over and put a hand on my shoulder. She was slightly red faced.

"I am really sorry. I had no idea it was that fool of a dog who caused all this. Wow! From now on, I'll make sure he's locked up or tied up when I go into the stable. You see, I was a little late today, many of the horses were supposed to be out by eight, so I'm afraid I forgot about the dog for a while," she said, looking very embarrassed.

"But do you have any idea where Redrose went?" she said, changing the subject. *How typical*, I thought. *She doesn't even thank me for helping out!* I shrugged my shoulders and was going to ignore her, but out of consideration for the horse, I took a deep breath and said, "I don't really have a clue where she might have gone. I was supposed to be on a trail ride with Pia right now, but she hasn't shown up yet, so I might as well help you find her."

An awkward silence fell over the stable area. Even the chirping of the birds seemed to pause.

Just then, a car came racing up the driveway. It stopped briefly in front of the stable, made a u-turn and left again.

"Who...?!" started Anette, but then we saw a girl standing in the cloud of dust from the car. It was Pia! She came running toward us, looking flushed and worked up. She was waving her arms and screaming:

"What happened? What *happened*?"

I barely had enough time to think, *How does she know something happened*? before Pia continued shouting, "Redrose is running down the highway!"

Chapter 3

"WHAT?!" Anette and I screamed at the same time, and Pia quickly explained.

"Well, you see, and I'm sorry, Julia, I was so late because we had to stop at Daddy's office on the way to pick up some 'important things' or whatever, so, so..." Pia stopped and took a deep breath before she continued.

"So we were driving pretty fast after that, and then I thought I was seeing things, because I thought I saw a horse running on the road, toward us! There were several other cars, and a few of them had stopped already. So I told Daddy to stop, and then I jumped out. That's when I saw it was Redrose, and I tried walking toward her. But of course –" Pia had gotten really angry at that point, "– a bunch of idiots started honking their horns, so she got scared and turned around. Then she started running the opposite way, the same way as the traffic! We couldn't really do anything but come up here..." she finished.

"Oh! The phone! Maybe..." Anette said over her shoulder before she disappeared into the stable to answer the ringing phone. Meanwhile Pia and I took Penny and

Prisci outside, since it was highly unlikely that we would have time to ride for a while.

"It was the police! They've gotten at least five phone calls about a horse running down the road. They've closed off parts of the highway and called a vet," shouted Anette as she came running back toward us.

"A vet? A *vet*?? What do they need a *vet* for?" I screamed. I was definitely not in the right state of mind to draw sensible conclusions. Anette looked at me sympathetically, and said, slowly and clearly, as if I was stupid or something, "To shoot a tranquilizer at her, of course, so that they can catch her. Let's go!"

With pockets full of treats, a bridle and a lead rope, we got into Anette's old car with a trailer in tow, and took off. At the police barrier we explained who we were and they let us through. After a little while we were informed of the situation. A large veterinary van, a farrier's car and a trailer, plus two police cars formed a barrier around Redrose, who was panic-stricken as she ran between the cars, trying to find a way out. Every time she looked like she might try to jump over the lowest part of the barrier, a police officer would get in the way, yelling and waving his arms at her.

After we stopped the car and walked closer, we could see that the poor mare was covered in sweat and foam, and you could see the white parts of her eyes. She was rearing and stepping around nervously, and I noticed that the vet and the farrier were talking anxiously to a police officer. They all seemed relieved at the sight of us, and Anette told them she would try to calm the horse down.

"You'd better be careful – she's completely crazy!" exclaimed one of the policemen, while the vet looked skeptically at him.

"I wonder what *they* did to try to calm her down," I muttered to Pia, and we both rolled our eyes.

Anette slowly approached the nervous horse. She walked very calmly, holding a bridle and lead rope behind her back while reaching the other hand filled with treats out in front of her. Redrose flapped her ears at the sound of Anette's soothing voice, which she associated with food and being turned out to green enclosures. Anette stopped and looked down at the ground, just peeking at the horse briefly now and then. At this point Redrose stood quite still, looking hesitantly at Anette. Finally she walked over to her, eagerly chowed down the carrot pieces, and seemed happy to finally see someone familiar, who understood her. Anette sneakily slipped the bridle onto the mare's head and started stroking her neck, while the horse slowly lowered its noble head. I heard a sigh of relief go through the group of onlookers, and then Anette said, "I think we can try to get her on the trailer without tranquilizers. Of all the horses at the stable, this mare is usually the easiest one to load in the trailer."

Pia and I hurried over to Anette's trailer, unbolted the doors and lowered the ramp slowly. We opened the door in front too, to make the trailer seem lighter. Anette led the horse in a few circles, before she set a course for the ramp. Redrose hesitated, and then reared a little in front of the ramp and neighed loudly. Anette just whispered to her, then stepped up on the ramp as she enticed the horse with more treats. Redrose followed her, and three minutes later she was securely tied to the trailer and eating some hay. Every so often, she jerked nervously as she glanced around, but mostly she was surprisingly calm considering what she had just been through.

As Redrose was being examined by the vet, Anette peeked into the car.

"Ouch! I checked the odometer before we left, and it looks like Redrose may have run over *three miles* on the tarmac!" Pia and I both moaned. What would Redrose's owner say?

"Well, this will most likely take a toll on her legs," said the vet. "They're a little stiff right now, and I saw some cracks in her hooves. I recommend that you call your own farrier as soon as you get home. She shouldn't be ridden for at least a couple of days. However, it's important to walk her on a lead rope and preferably do a little stretching over the next two days to make sure her legs aren't *completely* damaged." he concluded with a worried expression.

"She'll be able to jump again, won't she?" asked Pia, who had been thinking the same thing as I; Redrose's owner loved to jump and was an active competitor at events. Also, Redrose loved to jump and rarely yielded to a hurdle.

The vet shrugged his shoulders. Clearly, he didn't like the question, but then he seemed to pull himself together. "Sure. She should be able to jump again. She should be back to normal within a week or so. If not, a vet should look at her again."

We both sighed with relief.

When we finally got back to the stables, it was well after ten o'clock, and Linn's Stable was in a state of total chaos. In our rush to rescue Redrose, we had, naturally, forgotten to leave a message about what was going on and where we were, so the group of bewildered people that met us in the farmyard wasn't exactly friendly. Michelle, Redrose's twenty-four year old owner, and Eline, Chestnut's owner, were in the middle of a heated discussion with Linn, and neither of them looked too happy. In addition, there was a bunch of other people in riding clothes standing around, deep in agitated conversation with each other. At our arrival they all stopped and turned around, and the scene appeared downright funny. Most of them rushed toward us as soon as we had parked.

"*What in the world is going on?!* WHERE have you been?" yelled Linn loudly, looking both stern and worried at the same time, something that was very uncharacteristic of her. Anette signaled for Pia and me to unload Redrose, and then she started explaining everything that had happened.

Just as she got started, Eline came striding toward her with an angry expression on her face, and burst out, "Why was Chestnut in the wrong stall?!"

The three of us from the "expedition" looked at her in surprise. Then it came to me... In all the upheaval I had momentarily forgotten that I had just let the stallion into the first empty stall.

"And WHY has my horse not been turned out, as

is clearly stated in the contract?" asked another horse owner angrily.

"And Gollum is not supposed to go in that tiny little enclosure over there!" commented somebody else. Soon there was such a ruckus that nobody could hear what anybody said. Pia and I glanced at each other, and as we were about to lead Redrose out of the trailer, Michelle came and grabbed the lead rope out of our hands. Anette saw it, and then said loudly, "Please, everybody! Listen up!"

At first nobody could even hear what she was trying to say, but she has a pretty strong voice when she wants to, and eventually they all fell silent and let her speak. "I am terribly sorry about all this, but it *is* the unfortunate truth that everything that's wrong happened because I was stupid enough to let my dog, Rajsaj, loose while I fed the horses this morning. Somehow, he managed to open the doors to some of the stalls before Julia here realized what he'd done and managed to catch him as well as the horses who then got out. The horses that got loose were Chestnut, Gollum, Firefly and Coliseum. Unfortunately Redrose managed to run away, but that's a story I'll tell you, Michelle, privately. I will take care of everything that is out of place as soon as I can." With that, she went with Michelle into the stable.

"Orange juice, please," I said with a smile to the flight attendant, who politely smiled back. She poured the juice into a plastic cup and handed it to me before continuing down the aisle with her cart. I had to laugh to myself as I continued thinking about what happened after the runaway incident at the stable.

After having talked to Anette, Michelle had come up to Pia and me, looking a little embarrassed. She apologized for her behavior earlier and thanked us for having helped get Redrose back unharmed. Fortunately, Redrose didn't suffer any lasting damage, and the two of them actually placed first at a small club event in show jumping only two weeks later! The picture I was holding in my hand of the delighted pair was actually from that event.

Cecilie broke off my daydream by telling me to fasten my seatbelt, because we were coming in for a landing soon. After getting out of the plane, waiting for our luggage for a long time, and then searching for the right bus, we finally arrived at our condo resort in Alcudia.

"Man, is it hot!" exclaimed Cecilie, stopping to roll up her jeans, which were way too warm for such weather. It was overcast, but the air was still hot and humid. Outside the reception area, I noticed a thermometer which showed 36 degrees Celsius, almost 90 degrees Fahrenheit. Tropical vacation, here we are!

After getting the keys to our condo, and arguing all the way to a room with a bed and luggage space, we were finally happy. That kind of bickering is all part of the fun of our family's traveling, so none of us takes it too seriously.

"That pool outside sure looks inviting! How about it, Julia, do you want to go for a swim?" asked Cecilie excitedly as she rummaged through her suitcase looking for a swimsuit.

"I have to admit that sounds pretty wonderful right now, so yes, I do!" I answered, wiping sweat off of my forehead. We quickly changed into our swimsuits and ran playfully to the pool. After stopping briefly under an icy cold shower we dove into the beautiful, turquoise water. It felt great! A couple of cute boys were sitting on the edge of the pool, and Cecilie started splashing water and acting more cheerful and giddy than I had seen her for a long time. Reluctantly I had to admit to myself that the next two weeks might just turn out pretty well after all...

After a very refreshing swim and some play fighting with my sister, I pulled myself up on the edge of the pool. Cecilie was a real fish, swimming and diving and having a great time in the water. I only saw short glimpses of her whenever she came up to the surface for air. If I hadn't known any better, I might have mistaken her for a dolphin.

As I let my legs splash in the water, my thoughts wandered back to another swim story... *I guess it must have been over a year ago now? What a day that was!*

Chapter 4

"Are you almost ready?" Pia dangled her legs impatiently back and forth by Prisci's chest. The pony grazed calmly a short distance away from the tethering post, her gray ears flapping, and she lifted her head every so often to look around curiously. Pia pretended to be utterly bored, lying down on her pony's bare back, and Prisci just continued to eat. With her shoes at the root of the tail and her elbows resting on Prisci's shoulders, she yawned big and demonstratively.

"You don't have to exaggerate! I know perfectly well that you're not that comfortable up there," I laughed out loud, but started brushing a little faster.

"And *you* don't have to polish that pony as if it was going to a show, do you?" Pia grinned and got up from the rather uncomfortable position. Carefully she grabbed the reins to the bridle, which was a very basic one without a noseband, touched it to her sensitive horse's mouth, and shot forward in a gallop into the hilly field right behind the stable. I gave a sigh and smiled. Pia was so full of energy!

As I put on Penny's bridle she started stepping in anticipation, and I threw a glance at Pia on her pony as they raced uphill in the grass. Prisci made a little bow before she sped up, and I thought I heard something like a "Yeehaw!"

In no time at all, they were at the top of the hill, where the jumping arena is, and they disappeared behind a cluster of trees. Quickly, I pulled on my helmet and a backpack, jumped up on my lively, black steed and kicked her into a trot in pursuit of my friend. Penny started a fast trot, lifting her legs high, and begged to be allowed to run. I got her down to a slow trot before I kicked off in a gallop and we raced up the grassy hill. She galloped evenly, and I enjoyed the mild summer wind on my face and the feeling of flying forward, but I kept a firm grip on her mane as my thighs clung tightly to her sides. Have you ever tried to gallop bareback uphill on a skinny pony?

It didn't take long before we reached the top and hit the forest trail. Then I burst out laughing. On the ground behind a tree was Pia, with her tongue hanging out of her mouth and a wild look in her eyes. But she was holding on tightly to Prisci's reins, who whinnied sweetly toward her friend. Pia sat up with a mock offended look as she said, "You're *laughing* at the sight of your best friend lying dead on the ground?!"

"I guess I am! Maybe it has something to do with the fact that one of her legs was stomping so impatiently!" I laughed and rode Penny in a trot in amongst the trees.

"Hey, wait for me!" called Pia. I turned around and

started laughing again. Prisci was trotting more or less sideways, with Pia at her side, huffing and puffing.

"Let me see you jump up, then!" I teased.

"Easy – for – you – to – say!" huffed Pia as she continued to run. But then she managed to throw herself onto the pony's back, and soon they ran past us, right where the trail widened into a narrow dirt road. I let Penny start galloping and we caught up with them pretty easily. The two mares galloped evenly and peacefully side-by-side without rivalry, and we took it easy as well. We didn't want to wear them out, but it's always more comfortable to gallop than to trot on a slim, short-legged pony!

Suddenly, both ponies were pointing their ears, so we let them slow down to a walk. Then we heard hoofbeats, and a moment later Nikita and her owner appeared around the bend. The bay mare, who was actually very beautiful, had sweat trickling down her forehead, and she was foaming lightly around her neck, trotting off balance. The rider, Martine, instantly pulled hard on the reins while sitting up in a light seat when she saw us. The pony tried to open its mouth and stuck its head up in order to avoid the pain, but was prevented by the noseband and a tight, firm martingale.

The two of them had been at Linn's Stable for about a year now, and Nikita was in the process of changing from a calm and trusting pony, who used to walk beautifully on long reins and could jump sky high, into a very nervous creature with unbalanced steps and movements. *Thanks to her owner…!* I thought accusingly. I saw the horse's eyes rolling in her head as they passed us, and Martine nodded briefly before she spurred the horse so hard its tail whipped and it jumped forward into a jerky trot.

"Honestly, I'd like to give that girl a taste of her own spurs and whip!" hissed Pia as we both stared at the pair. I smiled at my friend's angry outburst, but totally agreed with her. We both entered into a, if I may say so, well-deserved bashing of Martine.

"I have every respect for pro riders who use spurs carefully and sensibly, but people like *her* shouldn't be allowed to have them at all! To abuse spurs to the extent that she does means she obviously doesn't have a clue how they're supposed to be used."

"I agree! Actually, I don't know why that girl has a horse," grumbled Pia, "She doesn't even seem to *like* her pony."

"That's for sure! The way she treats that sweet, beautiful animal, you'd think she doesn't like horses at all! I've never heard Martine praise Nikita, and she never says anything nice *about* her horse either," I continued.

After we had vented our frustration over Martine for a while, we switched to more pleasant topics. A little later, Penny and I took the lead off the dirt road, down a winding, almost invisible trail which, after a quarter mile or so, stopped by a very idyllic little pond. Pia and I sat on our horses for a while, just enjoying the pretty view and the peaceful surroundings. The dark blue water of the pond was almost completely still and shimmered toward us. The only thing you could hear was the pleasant sound of water gently splashing toward the sandy shore.

The pond was surrounded by trees, and it was as if the summer was glistening green in the sun, far away from civilization. This was one of my favorite places, and even on a nice, cold fall day it was really relaxing to stand there at the edge of the water and enjoy the scenery.

Pia, of course, had to go and interrupt this wonderful peace and quiet after only a few minutes.

Impatiently she asked, "Are we going in the water, or are we just going to stand around all day?" Prisci was impatient too, scraping her hoof on the ground, while Penny just stared at the water with pointed ears. That's when I first started realizing how a rider's behavior can often reflect on her horse...

"No, of course not! Let's go swimming. I'll race you!" I yelled, and gave Penny a kick to get started.

Pia just looked at me with surprise and shouted after me, "Hey, you're not going swimming with your clothes on, are you?"

Laughing, I started to rein in Penny slowly, not realizing we were already at the water's edge. She had other plans, however, and stopped shorter than I expected, her feet already in the water, while I went sailing through the air, landing head first in the pond!

Pia trotted her pony to my rescue, and reached us quickly in order to give me a hand up. Prisci obviously wasn't going one step further in the icky wet stuff than she had to and *she* stopped short too, causing Pia to land as unceremoniously in the pond as I just had!

We both screamed when we hit the cold water (I'm telling you, the water in Norway is not particularly warm

34

on an early morning in June!), and scrambled back up on the shore as fast as we could. Our ponies looked at us in shock, turned and started running straight for the woods! Pia and I exchanged worried looks, and then quickly ran after them on the pine needle-covered forest floor.

Visions of horrifying scenes went through my head. Visions of Penny stepping on her reins and tearing her mouth, and Penny ...

"Oh no, how could we have been so careless?" I shouted with Pia running next to me. I felt hot and cold at the same time, and my heart beat so hard it seemed as if my brain had stopped.

Suddenly I saw something, and I shot my arm out to stop Pia. She frowned and was about to push back, but I signaled for her to be quiet as I nodded in the direction of the trail. Then we both stared at something moving behind a grove of trees, and started walking slowly. Pia went past me, and when she disappeared behind a tree I heard her start talking. For a brief second I worried that maybe Pia had gone crazy from the shock, but then I became hopeful. Was she talking to the ponies?

Limping forward, I soon reached a nice little clearing full of green grass, which still showed traces of the morning dew, and there were the ponies, grazing peacefully. I let out a deep sigh of relief, and some of the tension in my body vanished. Pia quickly grabbed hold of Prisci's reins, and the gray mare waved her ears slightly as she looked at me with brief interest before continuing to eat. Penny grazed rapidly and effectively, as if she knew that she'd be taken away from this wonderful place soon. Calmly, I walked toward her. At first she moved away a little, but then she changed her mind and, to my delight, took a couple of steps toward me. Moving very slowly, I grabbed the reins, and then all the remaining tension gave out and I breathed freely again.

"Geezers capreezers, that was nerve-wracking!" Pia burst out. She let Prisci continue to graze while she examined her horse's legs thoroughly.

"Don't even mention it! That was one close call!" I said, loud and relieved. Then I started doing the same as Pia, and fortunately we both established that the ponies had not been hurt. Pia jumped up on Prisci's back and started stroking her lovingly on the neck. I led Penny around a little, to make sure she was okay, before I too jumped up and we rode the ponies at a walk back to the little beach. This time, despite the fact that our clothes were already soaked, we decided it would be best to wear our bathing suits, so we changed quickly.

"I think we'd better approach slowly and let them take the time they need," I suggested, and Pia nodded in agreement.

So we walked the horses leisurely toward the water, on half reins, and then let them sniff curiously at the water's light lapping at the shore. Prisci snorted so hard that some drops of water got sprayed into her nose. She was pretty funny; she looked so surprised, and then she stared at the water with her ears pointed to the extreme. Penny stared in fascination too. Then she started scraping with her hoof, making the water splash. We had a good laugh at our cute little ponies, and we gradually tried to lure them further into the water. Neither of us had gone swimming with a horse before, nor had our ponies been in contact with any water other than their drinking or bath water or when they'd jump a little brook in the woods. This was new territory for all four of us.

After a while we rode further in, slowly but gradually, getting out far enough for the water to reach their hocks. Pia and I exchanged eye contact, unsure about whether or not to continue.

"Um..." started Pia. "Maybe we ought to leave it at this for now, and try again some other time?" I nodded and turned Penny around.

"They did pretty well though, considering it was a first!" Besides, the water was way too cold, we told ourselves as we tried to get dressed holding onto the horses.

We went swimming several times that summer, I remember. On one of the warmer days in July, even the horses went swimming, and we had a blast in the refreshing water. Eventually our ponies learned to love swimming. It didn't take long before we were doing exactly what we had been envisioning from the start, trotting into the water at full speed with water splashing to the sides and the horses whinnying contentedly. It served as a lesson that we usually can't start out expecting our heart's desire, but have to take things in little steps to reach a goal.

Chapter 5

I suddenly jumped from the shock of something icy landing on my stomach. We had been in Spain for almost a week, and I was lying on a chaise lounge at the beach, trying to both work on a tan and avoid heat stroke.

"Ugh! What…?" I screamed, looking up to see Cecilie standing over me with a big grin on her face. Despite the unpleasant shock, I was happy to discover that the cold thing on my stomach was a big piece of melon. "M-mm…!"

Cecilie plopped down on the seat next to me, as she watched the people on the beach from behind her big, expensive sunglasses. With one hand she slowly stroked her fingers through her long, blonde hair, making it fall softly over her cheeks, as she stretched her long, tanned legs. Her dark blue and green two-piece swimsuit looked really good on her. That wasn't a surprise though, seeing as how everything looked good on her. It's kind of funny how some people can make any piece of clothing they put on look really good! Paris Hilton, for instance, would look good dressed in a trash bag according to some magazines, and it's probably not far from the truth.

I stroked a hand quickly through my strawberry blonde, shoulder-length hair while glancing down at my own modest body. Quickly I lay back down to make my stomach look as flat as possible. Luckily, I had finally started getting a tan, and I was proud of my tan lines.

"Looking forward to tonight, are you?" Cecilie looked at me with a teasing expression as she took a bite of her melon.

"Sure, I just hope it'll be fun," I answered with a smile. Cecilie couldn't care less about horses, so she was going to stay back in our rental condo, while my parents and I were going on an excursion to a horse ranch.

"What about you, are you going to stay in tonight?" I asked, raising my eyebrows at her. Cecilie put on an innocent-looking expression.

"*Me?* How can you suspect *me* of doing anything sneaky? I'm as innocent as an angel! I'm going to stay here all by myself, read the paper and go to bed at nine!" she said convincingly. Within three seconds we both burst out laughing, but deep down I was a little worried about what Cecilie might actually be planning. The truth was that my sister was quite a party girl, and I had been forced to tell white lies before to make my parents think that she was asleep in her bed all night, when in fact she'd been at a party and sneaked back in through the window at 4 a.m.

I've got to stop worrying about her. She'll probably be just fine, I told myself. *After all, she's sixteen! She must know what to do and what not to do*. With that in mind,

I ate the rest of my melon and wondered what my own night would be like.

"Wow! What a beautiful place!" exclaimed my mom as we stepped out of the bus that had taken us and a bunch of other people to a large ranch on the island of Mallorca. At the ranch we were, according to the brochure, supposed to ride, barbeque, and play cowboys – and to tell the truth we were all just a little apprehensive about exactly how corny this was going to be.

"Yeah! It looks great!" I said smilingly as we started walking to the main house along with all the people from two full buses. The person who greeted us was a rather chatty, scrawny-looking kid, all decked out in chaps and spurs, which spun and clattered as he walked. *I hope he doesn't ride with those!* I thought to myself. He welcomed everyone. Then he told us about the various riding options, including a wagon ride for those who didn't want to ride horseback. Another large group of people had apparently finished their ride, and they were sitting in the sun on big log benches on the terrace.

While I helped my parents find suitable helmets, I wondered anxiously what kind of horse I would get and how this was all going to work out.

"Ha, ha! This will be fun, don't you think?" Dad was laughing out loud while trying to press a tiny helmet, which was clearly too small, down over his graying brown hair. I giggled as I handed him a bigger helmet, and then we walked down a small hill toward the horses.

My mouth fell open for a minute. I I had never seen so many horses in one place before! There were long, solid tethering posts, and there must have been at least twenty horses standing by each post! All of them were already saddled and just stood there, dozing in the evening sun. To the left of the tethering posts the landscape consisted of completely flat and open fields, with only a few bushes here and there. To the right was a small brick stable building, with a long watering hose and some hay bales in front. Right behind it we saw five paddocks, and three of them had horses in them, who were snatching up bits of hay from the ground. My guess was that those horses had the day off.

The whole busload of people gathered around the tethering posts, and a couple of the wranglers got busy dividing us into groups and assigning a horse to each of us. Smiling, I waved my parents over to the beginner group, and then I threw a long glance at the guy who was assigning horses to our group. He looked like he was no more than 17 years old, tall and blonde, and extremely tan. Aah! – he was really cute!

"How long have you been riding?" he asked.

"Abb… About six years," I answered in stuttering English. "I have my own pony," I added.

He gave a slight nod and yelled, "Blue Eye for this girl!"

My horse was dark brown, and before I mounted I glimpsed a triangular-shaped blaze by the muzzle. When I bent down, I could see that he had white socks on his feet. He stood calmly among all the horses and people who were crowding the place, with one ear turned back toward me.

A friendly looking, brown-haired girl loosened the reins of the bay horse from the post and handed them to me. I barely had time to let the horse sniff my hand before I was thrown into the saddle. *Whoa! What an enormous horse!* I thought as I settled myself in the seat.

Two other horses started backing up right toward us, so I quickly rode to the side so that I wouldn't be in the way. I stroked Blue Eye on the neck and tried to get to know him a little, and had just enough time to adjust the stirrups before we were ready to start.

At first it felt different sitting so high up. After all, I was used to riding a pony that was probably about 12 inches shorter! But it didn't take long to get used to Blue Eye's long and even steps. As we moved forward at a walking gait, I noticed that several of the riders around me were trying to get their horses to collect themselves, and some of the horses were actually walking with a nice movement in their hind legs and lifting their backs a little. I was inspired to work on Blue Eye too, because I could tell he was holding his back somewhat low and his head stiff and high. Carefully I picked up the reins, used the leg aids and my seat to ask him to collect himself, and then wriggled the reins softly in order to position him. To my surprise he responded very well. I noticed that his steps got more resilient, which made it more comfortable to ride him, and he held his neck very nicely. After a while he walked in a collected and even manner on semilong reins, with only the help of my weight and leg aids, and I smiled triumphantly.

Another boy who had been running around helping people mount up took the lead, riding on a beautiful pinto that stood out significantly from the rest of the horses. I steered Blue Eye and after we had been riding for a while I turned around and smiled in amazement. There must have been about thirty riders! It would be fun to ride with that many people – I had never done that before.

"He valks verry nice! You arre cleverr," said the rider behind me, who could see us really well as we came around a curve. It was a grown woman with brown hair gathered in a ponytail underneath her helmet, and she smiled at me. I said thanks and smiled back, and then we chatted a little as we rode. Suddenly, I sat up straight in the saddle again, because apparently we had changed to a trot! Blue Eye trotted on and I made myself more comfortable, shortening the reins. *Darn it!* I thought and made a face. *My capris are causing the stirrup straps to chafe. I should have worn jeans. But that would have been so hot!*

After a while we slowed down to a walk again, and a wrangler went galloping past us on an impressive, black horse and exchanged a few words with the cute guy up front. I was surprised to see that none of the horses in the line moved so much as an ear, so I guess they were used to this. If one of the horses back home had thundered past Chestnut, for instance, it wouldn't have gone over very well...

The wrangler on the black horse then turned his horse around and galloped past us back the way he had come. Our group leader shortened his reins, turned and yelled as his beautiful pinto quickly backed up, "Everyone ready for a little cantering?"

"Yes!" I yelled enthusiastically along with the rest of the riders.

"All right! Don't let your horse pass the one in front of you – keep the line going! Here we go...!" At that he turned his pinto around and, with one hand on the reins, kicked off in a canter. The rest of us had no choice but to follow, as we were on a narrow trail and all the horses followed each other in a line at the same speed. I gave Blue Eye a kick and he took off in a bumpy canter. As I looked around briefly, I noticed that most of the horses had their heads down or held high, and clearly wanted to stay behind the horse in front of them. Many of the riders were making intense facial expressions as they tried to calm their horses down, me included, and so we were all pretty shocked when our group leader suddenly stopped on the spot and asked if everything was going okay. *Yeah, everything was fine until now!* I wanted to tell him.

Goodness gracious, how chaotic! I thought, and couldn't help giggling while I looked around. The stop had come so suddenly that only a few of us had managed to stop our horses in time. That's why about five or six horses and riders were now standing side-by-side, muzzles and behinds in all directions. Some of the riders looked kind of worried while others were busy trying to keep their horses from eating the green bushes we had stopped right next to. It was typical for me to start laughing in a situation like this! I always have to laugh when things get out of control, when others usually frown. I didn't get to laugh for long, however, because just as suddenly as we had stopped we started up again. We all managed to get into a nice line again, and when we slowed down to a trot and moved onto a sandy trail between small, green trees, I gazed at the beautiful surroundings and realized that I was actually enjoying this experience.

Our group ride was nearing the end, but apparently we still had another gallop in store. This one was going to be faster, so those who wished to were given the opportunity to switch over to the "trotting group," which we had just caught up with. A surprising number of riders chose to switch groups, while I didn't even consider it. I rarely decline a chance for a fast gallop! Besides, the horse I was riding was very well behaved and obedient, so I figured I didn't have anything to worry about. With the cute wrangler and his pinto up front, we halted and once again ended up in a big pile, so to speak – a little smaller this time. I started wondering if he was doing it on purpose, just to check if we were paying attention. He asked if we were ready, then turned and kicked his horse into a trot almost before we had a chance to answer.

I noticed a girl who evidently had a more difficult horse. It was jumping and bouncing around, suddenly trotting out from the line while holding its head high. It even managed to stumble on a big rock before the girl finally got it under control and steered it back into line. Then we were off on a gallop!

As we thundered forward I rose up in the saddle. Blue Eye pulled on the reins, then pulled his head down toward the ground and showed signs of bucking. I nipped lightly at the reins as I squeezed firmly with my leg aids, and that set him back to normal again. I smiled – it's always fun when an otherwise well-behaved horse tries a few tricks and then lets itself be corrected and goes back to its usual obedient behavior.

After we were safely back at the ranch, the wranglers came around and helped us tie up the horses. I cuddled with Blue Eye briefly and thanked him for the ride. While I was standing there stroking his forehead, I thought that, surprisingly enough, he didn't really feel too big for me. I actually felt as if I sat on him really well! This almost scared me a little – the thought that my own pony back home was so much smaller. Was I... ? No, I didn't want to think about it!

Just then another group rode into the farmyard. It was the beginners, which mostly consisted of small children, and my parents and people their age, and they all seemed to be in high spirits. I walked over to my parents and held their horses as they dismounted. Then a wrangler came over and took the horses away. Until now, I hadn't actually noticed what the horses looked like. I took a better look at the two closest to me. One of them had several surface wounds and scrapes, and had a kind of square-ish shape. By that I mean that its hipbones were sticking out from its body and the cross was narrow. With the lightest touch on the flank with my finger, I could feel its ribs. The other horse was rounder and looked a little better, but it also had wounds.

"Did you have a nice ride?" I asked my parents, pulling myself away from the horses. Neither my mom nor my dad had ever ridden much before. I was the only one in the family with a special interest in horses.

"Yeah, it was fun," said Dad with a laugh as he took off his helmet and stroked a hand through his hair to fix it. We continued talking as we walked toward the terrace.

"Fortunately our group kept to a walk the whole time," smiled my mom. "That's probably a good thing since most of the riders in our group had never ridden before!"

Next we were told that we'd have some time to ourselves before dinner, so I decided to walk around a little and look at the horses. I went down to the tethering posts where the wranglers were busy unsaddling the horses and taking them out to the paddocks. Each of them was actually leading five horses at a time, and all these horses were walking nicely in a cluster! I couldn't help being impressed by this, and wondered if they were behaving this nicely because they viewed the wranglers as their leaders and therefore didn't argue with them, or if they were simply so tired that they didn't have the energy to argue... I was hoping it was the first reason.

Right by the paddocks was a large tree, which I assumed provided some precious shade when the sun was at its hottest during the day. Tethered to the tree were two cute little Shetland ponies. I went over to say hello to them and they looked at me with interest. Then I walked slowly along the fence of the paddocks, watching all the horses. I was relieved to see that most of them looked sound, without any visible injuries.

I stopped, as one of the horses caught my eye. It was a good-looking, red mare, which was standing a few yards away from me, resting. A special blaze adorned her face, starting by her left eye and ending by the right nostril. The mare reminded me a lot of a horse I had seen at Linn's Stable only a week ago, and my mind wandered off again...

Chapter 6

"Did you hear? Some mare is coming over to visit Chestnut today." Michelle looked up at me from a squatting position as she cleaned a small wound on Redrose's leg.

"Oh, really? No, I didn't know," I answered and paused my brushing of Prisci. Pia had already left for her summer vacation, and I was looking after Prisci for her until I left for Spain in a couple of days.

"That's what I've been told. Apparently he's very popular as a stud, which I guess explains why Eline hasn't had him castrated. I'm sure such matings make for a little extra income for the stallion owner..."

"Probably. I've also heard he used to be a very good racehorse. Apparently he won several international events, so there are probably a lot of people who want to have their mares covered by him," I said, continuing with the grooming. A whole handful of gray, soft coat hairs came loose from the brush and floated slowly away in the warm, almost still-standing air. Michelle put the aloe vera spray back in her kit and stroked her horse lovingly on the neck.

"Yeah, I'm sure," she nodded, and giggled as Redrose nipped her hair lightly with her muzzle. I smiled at the sight of them, but turned instantly when I heard a loud engine in the driveway.

"That's her now, I bet! This I've got to see!" exclaimed Michelle. She loosened Redrose from the tethering post, and put her in the paddock nearby. I quickly finished grooming Prisci and took her to Stable B, because there wouldn't be an available paddock for her and Penny for about an hour.

When I came back out, there was a nice big van in the farmyard, with an equally large trailer behind it. I saw Eline standing there, talking to a man who had evidently just jumped out of the van, plus a couple of riders who had gathered around the trailer. I went over and joined them, and shortly after, the man came around to open the door and lower the ramp.

"Here's my grand dame," he said proudly, nodding toward the trailer. A beautiful, noble Thoroughbred glanced at us from the trailer, her ears pointed and nostrils vibrating slightly. She was a chestnut, with a special blaze winding down her face from her left eye to right nostril. The man, who was tall and thin and looked as if he might be in his forties, went into the trailer and led the horse out. She backed down the ramp calmly, and looked around curiously once she had her hooves safely planted on the ground. Then she let out an ear-splitting neigh.

"C'mon Cissy, try not to burst my eardrums, will you?" the man scolded lovingly, stroking her soothingly on the neck.

"Well, Tom, we welcome Cissy to her home for the next couple of days. Let's hope her visit has a happy result," said Eline, winking knowingly. Michelle and I exchanged surprised looks, because we weren't used to such a cheery comment from Eline, who was usually so sulky. *Maybe she's more cheerful around people her own age?* I wondered.

"Go ahead and put her in the pasture over there. That's Chestnut's field, where he receives his lady friends," Eline continued humorously, and pointed. Once again I raised my eyebrows in complete amazement at Eline's cheerfulness. Then my attention was drawn to the mare, which was definitely a gorgeous creature. From what I could see, she had a very good conformation with a nice neck and straight, muscular legs. Her back looked strong, and her mane was well defined.

"Guess I'd better go and get that lucky boy of mine then," said Eline, smiling at me. I gave her a friendly smile back.

"Gee, what's happening to Eline?" Michelle blurted out once the woman was out of earshot. I shrugged my shoulders.

"Maybe everybody has a lighter side, and maybe hers comes out when it's time for her horse to meet a girlfriend?" I suggested with a giggle, and Michelle laughed out loud. Accompanied by Camilla and Anette, we walked over to Chestnut's pasture. It was always fun to watch when he was first let out to meet a mare. Inside the pasture the mare's owner, Tom, was taking off the big transport covers from her legs and replacing them with lighter leg protectors. Then he removed the lead rope and came over to the gate where we were standing.

"This may seem a little too cautious, I guess. I'm not usually the overprotective mother hen around my horses, but in this particular case, when a mare is in a new place and meeting a temperamental stallion, I prefer to give her a little extra protection," he explained. And we nodded understandingly.

"She's absolutely gorgeous," said Camilla, admiring the horse as it trotted around with long steps and tall leg lifts. The red, well-groomed coat practically glistened in the sunlight. It was easy to see that Tom enjoyed the praise, as he gave us a big smile.

"Yeah, she's very pretty, if I may say so myself. And a good racehorse too, actually. I'm not really very active when it comes to racing, because I think it too easily becomes a ruthless exploitation of the horses. Cissi started her first race when she was three. She won it by a good margin, and since then she's done ten races of which she placed first in nine," he bragged. It wasn't meant to be arrogant, I think, but just showed how proud he was of his horse.

"That's very impressive! How old is she now?" I asked curiously.

"She's a real lady now, turned nine this winter, so I figured it was time for her to have a foal."

I nodded, and then the five of us turned as we heard a loud neigh behind us. The neigh came from Chestnut, who apparently had worked hard to control himself while walking next to Eline. She was leading him on a regular nylon halter and demanded just the same manners from him as she always did. He was expected to walk next to her on a loose line, without passing. His pent-up energy, along with the fact that he knew he wasn't supposed to pass his owner, caused him to trot at low speed, with an impressive collection, while snorting powerfully.

"There's the star now!" commented Tom, and didn't hide how much he liked Chestnut. "I've kept an eye on that boy since he first set his beautiful hooves on a racetrack," he told us. Eline laughed and stopped her stallion, which was also wearing light leg protectors. She opened the gate and let the stallion, who was now stepping anxiously, inside. He ran off at a trot, with good bounce and hold in the hind legs. His neck had a natural curve, his long chestnut-colored mane and tail stood out from his body, with muscles rippling in the sunlight, and his coat glistened various shades of red. Nobody could deny that he was an impressive sight! We just stood there admiring Chestnut, and I think we were all awed by his magnificence!

We humans standing by the fence weren't the only ones fascinated by Chestnut's beauty and radiance. Cissi stood completely still, staring at her new pasture mate with pointed ears and strongly vibrating nostrils. When he trotted past the mare, Anette commented, "Isn't she kind of tall?"

Tom, who seemed to be pulled out of a trance by the question, cleared his throat loudly and answered, "Yes, she's pretty tall. She's 16.5 hands high, but I guess Chestnut isn't much taller than that."

Eline shook her head slowly, without taking her eyes off the horses. They were now head to head, snorting into each other's nostrils, with tensed necks and vigorous movements.

"She's well in heat by now, so I bet she'll fall in love instantly," Tom said with a smile.

"I'm glad we can do it this way, by allowing them to play freely and go at their own pace. Personally, I think too many horse owners tie up the mares and get them impregnated whether they want to or not," he continued with an angry wrinkle on his forehead. Eline nodded in agreement.

"I never let Chestnut cover a mare that way. That's one of the reasons I can keep him under control in any situation. He knows very well that he has to behave and show good manners if he wants to get something. Otherwise he risks a kick," she said, and I was thinking the two of them were so right. I hadn't really thought much about these things before.

"If she's in heat and he listens to her signals, and they have enough room to play around in and don't have shoes on, the chance of injury isn't really very high," added Eline. Tom nodded in total agreement, and the two of them remained by the fence talking and admiring their beautiful horses, while the rest of us walked back to continue our chores. But their words stayed with me.

I was pulled back to the present by a soft hand touching my shoulder and startling me. "Dinner is ready," said

Mom's voice enticingly. I caught a glimpse of a big table full of yummy-looking food. I smiled at her, threw one last glance at the horse, which just happened to look so much like Cissi, and walked with her back to the terrace.

The evening passed quickly. We ate a lot of delicious barbeque served by the wranglers, got to know a nice Swedish family, and had fun watching a mechanical bull riding contest. We also watched a beautiful sunset on the horizon, where the sun made the clouds glow in all shades of pink.

Later, when we were walking to the bus to go home, I noticed that the tethering posts were empty, and all the horses were in the paddocks, contentedly eating the hay that had been left out for them. I smiled and thought that these horses may possibly have a better life than many horses back home in Norway. Even though some of them were a little square and got a few superficial insect bites now and then, they also got to stay outside with their herd all day, and probably were ridden a lot, seeing as some of them obviously knew quite a few things and were well-trained. Wouldn't a life like that be better than standing alone in a stall 22 hours a day, regardless of how well you're fed and how many muscles you have?

Chapter 7

"I don't believe this!" My mom was clearly upset and trying to not yell. It was well past midnight when Mom, Dad and I got back to our rental condo, and we were knocking on the door – to no avail. We only had one key to the condo, and since we were going to be gone tonight, my parents had let Cecilie keep the key. But it seemed as if she had left – *with* the key – and we had no idea where she was.

This was exactly what I had been worried about all along, but naturally hadn't wanted to say anything to Mom and Dad about. I knew that Cecilie had made friends with another girl earlier that day, one that was two years older than she, which meant she was eighteen. And I had overheard something about a dance club at ten o'clock, and something like, "Marco will meet us at..." Discretely, I got my cell phone out and called my sister. It rang for a long time.

"Yeah? Hola!" shouted Cecilie on the other end. I could hear loud music and laughter in the background.

"Cecilie, where *are* you?" I hissed quietly. I heard

more laughter in the background, then the music became fainter while I heard the sound of footsteps. Evidently Cecilie was moving away from the dance floor or wherever she was.

"Jooliaa! Is that you?" she asked jokingly.

"Where's the key, Cecilie? We can't get in!" I didn't need to keep my voice down anymore, because my parents were standing right next to me anyway. "And where are you, by the way?" I added.

"The key is by... pink..." Both phones were suffering from bad signals, in addition to all the noise on Cecilie's end, so I couldn't hear what she was saying very well.

"Pink? What are you talking about?"

"The pink flowers! It's in the flower bed outside the door," she explained, as the signal was suddenly restored.

"Tell Mom and Dad that I'll be home around two or so!" she shouted into the phone.

"But..." I stammered, but the dial tone was my only answer.

Quietly, I closed my phone and put it back in my pocket. Then I squatted down by the bushes around our little patio and pushed aside some pink flowers. And there was, in fact, a key. I grabbed it, unlocked the door and sank onto the couch, holding my head in my hands. Mom and Dad followed me anxiously, waiting impatiently for me to tell them what was going on.

"I think she's at a dance club," I said quietly. I didn't feel like trying to come up with something else.

"A dance club?! Without asking us? That is completely unacceptable! Here we are, trusting her to stay home alone for one evening, hoping that she might get to know some nice girls to talk to around here, and then she just... Argh!" By now Mom was almost screaming, so Dad grabbed her firmly by the arm and sat down with her on the other couch.

"What exactly did she say, Julia? Why was she there? Who was she with?" Even though Dad had his voice under control, it wasn't hard to tell that he was worried sick.

"I don't know – don't ask me!" I burst out. Suddenly I was totally fed up with all of Cecilia's partying and lying and sneaking around. I decided then and there that I would never lie for her again. *From now on you can face the heat by yourself!* I thought, and felt surprisingly relieved.

"All she said was that she'll be home around two," I said firmly, and at that I left the room and went to the bathroom to get ready for bed.

Neither of my parents went to bed until Cecilie got home. She sneaked inside without making a sound, and neither Mom nor Dad said a word. But it was perfectly clear by the stern looks on their faces, that there would be consequences ...

And I was right. During our last week, Cecilie wasn't left alone for a second. As a kind of punishment, she had to hang around with us constantly. Whenever Cecilie and I were just going to the beach or the pool, I had strict orders to follow her wherever she went and not let her out of my sight. That wasn't so bad though, and she took it pretty well.

✳ ✳ ✳ ✳

"Well, people, how are we going to sum up this vacation?" asked Mom, while buttering a piece of bread. We were sitting outside our cozy, white condo eating breakfast.

"In a way I think these two weeks have gone extremely fast. I can't believe we're going home tomorrow!" answered Cecilie, spreading jelly on a piece of the lousy, white bread they sold at this place.

"One thing's for sure, I'm looking forward to going home and having a good, thick piece of whole grain bread with Norwegian brown cheese!" exclaimed Dad. We smiled at him, but we all agreed.

"No, but seriously..." started Dad, then thought about it. "It's not like we sat around and were lazy for two whole weeks, even if it's been relaxing, right?"

"Absolutely not! We rented a car for several days and toured Palma and Inca, and we got to see a lot of the fantastic nature they have here," said Mom enthusiastically.

"Not to mention a lot of shopping," said Cecilie with a big grin.

"And we went swimming at a lot of different beaches, big and little ones!" I continued.

"In the evenings, we went out to eat and we took long walks in the streets instead of sitting around at home..." started Dad.

"... and we went for a night swim!" I finished for him. Cecilie and I gave each other a big smile.

"Yeah, I guess we found out that it was pretty scary to go swimming at a beach in the dark when you can't see a thing," my sister said.

"It makes for a whole lot of screaming and nervous splashing," I giggled.

"So what should we do for our last two days? We have all of today and almost all of tomorrow, since our flight leaves late in the evening," said Mom. I already knew what I wanted to do, so I put on my most persuasive angel face as I looked at her and Dad.

"What about another visit to the horse ranch?" I suggested. "There's another tour scheduled for today, and (I looked briefly at my wrist watch) we still have about an hour to sign up before they close registration." My parents looked at each other, a rather doubtful look, and Cecilie objected loudly.

"I absolutely refuse to use my last day down here sweating around a bunch of stinky horses!" she said, with a disgusted look on her face.

"Take it easy, Cecilie, nobody's going to force you to do that," Mom said soothingly. "Julia, you know the ranch tour is pretty expensive, right? I hope you also know how much money we spend on you and horses in general..."

"Of course I do!" I said, struggling to keep up the angel face. I knew all too well that stable rent, riding lessons, vet bills, insurance and farrier costs all added up to *a lot* of money, and I was very grateful to my parents, who were paying for it all. In return I didn't get any allowance, but I still had some money from babysitting a couple of nights a week. I also knew that the stable where Penny was boarded was fairly expensive, because it had one indoor arena and two outdoor arenas in addition

61

to nice stable buildings, paddocks and pastures. The thought of it reminded me how lucky I was to have my own pony, and to be able to keep it in such a great place! Still smiling, though with a somewhat disappointed expression, I said, "I know how much money you spend on Penny and me, and it's okay if we have to drop the ranch idea today."

My mom immediately looked regretful, as if she had just caused an accident. She always looks like that when I'm cooperative and understanding. I think she actually feels guilty whenever I don't get my wishes!

"But maybe... honey, what do you think?" asked Mom, looking at Dad with raised eyebrows. Dad chewed on a piece of bread, and then eventually said, "If we're going to consider another ranch tour, I guess it goes without saying that Cecilie and one of us would stay behind while the other one goes with Julia."

I looked at Mom with renewed hope.

"To be honest, I actually liked the ranch tour a lot. I thought it was fun, and very scenic. Not to mention the good food and gorgeous sunset. If you don't mind, honey, I think that Julia and I could go and sign up," she finished by winking at me.

By now I was smiling from ear to ear. I couldn't help looking forward to riding a horse across the prairie again, and felt a pang of guilt when it occurred to me that I didn't really miss Penny as much as I thought I would. Of course I missed her! But truth be told, I hadn't actually thought that much about her during my vacation. *It's probably because you know she's safe and well taken care of. Besides, you'll see her on Wednesday, which is only two days from now!* I said firmly to myself, and pushed Penny out of my thoughts as I got ready to go to the beach before the much anticipated outing later in the day.

"Everyone ready to gallop?"

I laughed, shouted my answer enthusiastically, and kicked into a gallop on Diana, the smooth and flexible mare I was riding. *It sure feels wonderful to float away with such big steps, high above the ground!* I started in on my own thoughts. *Quit it! Small pony steps are much more fun and lively,* I said, trying to convince myself. To be thinking anything else was – in my opinion – a betrayal of Penny. Fortunately, riding required my concentration, and helped suppress these difficult thoughts and questions that were going through my mind. I was really enjoying the ride, which was at least as much fun as the last time. When I jumped down from Diana after returning to the ranch, I stroked her on the neck and thanked her for the ride.

Later, as I lay in bed trying to sleep through the last night in our rented condo, I tried to explain to myself that I hadn't betrayed Penny just because I enjoyed riding a bigger horse. Still, I couldn't put aside the question, which had been nagging at the back of my mind ever since I rode Blue Eye. Was I getting ready for a bigger horse? If so, could I have two horses at the same time?

C'mon, Julia, this is nonsense! It was my good, old conscience and loyalty to Penny that was stepping in.

You've already got a beautiful pony with great potential, and you haven't outgrown her yet – in any way, shape or form, my mind continued. Even so, I wasn't fully clear about what it was I wanted when my eyes finally fell shut, and my hand dropped the photo I had been looking at for the last fifteen minutes. It was a nice picture of Penny. It fell and landed silently on the floor.

Chapter 8

"Don't forget that you have a lot of unpacking and cleaning to do!" my mom shouted as I rolled my bike out of the driveway at our house. It was a little past eleven in the morning. After a good night's sleep back in my own bed in Norway and a quick breakfast, I was dying to get to the stable to see my sweet pony again.

"I know, I know! But I have all day! I simply *have* to go and see Penny *now*!" I said, and then I jumped on the bike and took off. With a glance over my shoulder as I left, I saw Mom shaking her head with a smile before she went back inside.

Oh, how wonderful it feels to be back again, I thought after the 15-minute bike ride to the stable. I stopped and took a deep breath of fresh, warm air before locking the bike to a tree by the driveway that led up to the stable, and then jogged the rest of the way. I said "hi" to several people I knew and chatted a little before going into Stable B to pick up Penny's halter. I was relieved to notice that the stable was empty and no horses were in their stalls. I hate seeing healthy horses standing inside in a stall when the weather is this nice. I walked up toward the pasture where Penny and her herd were, but when I caught sight of the ponies, I started running.

"Penny!"

Both Penny and Prisci, who were grazing contentedly side by side, lifted their heads instantly and looked curiously in my direction at the sound of my voice. I went through the gate and walked toward them a little before I stopped. Penny gave a low snort and started walking toward me. I got all warm and fuzzy inside, and started walking toward her again. When she reached me, I let her sniff my hand, which she nudged lightly, and then I gave her a big hug. Not exactly the dramatic reunion scene that I had pictured. You know, the kind of scene you might see in movies or read about in books, where the horse comes running at full speed toward its owner, whom it hasn't seen in a long time, and the owner goes running toward the horse with open arms. Then the owner jumps easily up on the back of the horse and they gallop off happily with mane and tail dancing in the wind... Okay, I admit it would have been pretty fun but it was a long shot!

"Geez, Penny! Did you shrink while I was gone?" I said teasingly and scratched her mane. It was wonderful to see her again! I took a step back in order to look at her properly. Was she really as big as before? *She has to be. Anything else would be impossible,* I answered myself. Was it me who had grown so much since then? Because I really did think she looked smaller than before. I decided to measure myself as soon as I got home. Calmly I pulled a carrot out of my pocket and broke off a piece. I offered it to Penny, who took it happily. *Well, one thing's for sure, you've grown back to your old size around the belly,* I reflected, smiling. Penny had filled out quite a bit during the two weeks she had spent outside, eating fresh grass.

Prisci, who was a couple of inches taller than Penny and somewhat more muscular, got pushy and started sniffing at my pants. I gave her a carrot too, before putting the halter on Penny's head and taking her with me. At the sudden sound of thumping hooves, I stopped and turned around. It was Pontus, Conny and Cilla. Until now, they had been standing in the shade under some big trees, but now they came running toward us. I smiled, and noticed Stine, who's Baldrian's exercise rider, leading the brown Cob horse up to the pasture.

The three galloping horses slowed down and stopped near Penny, me, and Prisci, who had followed us. Pontus stood a short distance away and was kind of showing off. His black coat shimmered in the sun, and his nostrils were vibrating and ears pointed so they almost met at the top as he paid close attention to what his friend was doing. He and Baldrian were almost as inseparable as Penny and Prisci, which had led to Conny and Cilla becoming good friends too.

Conny stuck her muzzle eagerly toward my pockets, but this was evidently too much for Penny. With her ears and mouth she told the other horse off. *This is my girl! Stay away from her!* Conny accepted the rebuke from the smaller pony and took a few steps toward Pontus instead. I smiled and continued leading Penny.

67

"Hi, Julia!" shouted Stine, as she opened the gate and took Baldrian inside.

"Hi! Long time no see!" I said, smiling at her. Stine closed the gate behind her before she pulled off her Cob's halter and patted him on the neck. His dark coat glistened over his strong, well-muscled body, and I guessed he had just had a shower. He ran off instantly, taking the lead in an elegant trot toward the shaded area under the trees, with the other horses following behind him.

"We've been taking our rides in the early morning these last few days," said Stine. "It's been so hot this week I can barely stand to do anything at all in the afternoon, especially riding. Of course, that's me," she added with a smile, patting her round belly.

"Oh, I'm with you! I just got back from Spain last night, and it's almost as hot here at home. I guess I'm going to brave the heat. We'll just go for a short, slow walk," I said, stroking Penny's neck lovingly. Stine opened the gate and held it open while I led my pony through.

"Miss Chubby here hasn't been ridden for two weeks, and the week before I left I was kind of tapering off gradually, so I'm afraid she's in pretty bad shape at the moment," I said, grinning at Stine. We walked downhill together and chatted the whole way.

"This can't be right," I muttered to myself. I had just stepped up on Penny, after having tightened the girth a few notches less than I usually did, and was somewhat puzzled. The stirrups felt uncomfortably short, and as I pulled them down a couple of notches, I was wondering why they were so different. I hadn't used the saddle for three weeks, because the last week before I left I had only been riding bareback. The question, which had first occurred to me while I was at the ranch in Mallorca, now came back with full force. *Had I really started outgrowing Penny?*

The answer came as I gently pushed my legs to make her move forward. Not only did my feet not even touch her stomach, but they were dangling *below* her stomach! I shook my head in confusion, and an overwhelming feeling that I can't describe rose up inside me. Shock, maybe. Disbelief. The feeling went through me like a wave, and I leaned forward over Penny's neck, closing my eyes tight. But I couldn't hold back the tears. They forced their way out and emerged out of the corner of my eyes. As I opened my eyes again, the tears trickled slowly down my cheeks. With blurry view I saw them land in Penny's thick mane, where they stayed briefly before vanishing.

"But how could this happen just like that, so suddenly?" I burst out in desperation, banging my fist on the kitchen table. My parents, who were sitting across from me, looked at each other. Then Mom started talking.

"You were probably a little too tall already before you left, sweetheart. You just didn't think about it. Now that you've ridden a bigger horse in Mallorca, and had a chance to feel how well those horses suited you, it's probably just a little strange to ride a small pony again."

"A small pony... You're saying it as if... as if..."
Frustrated as I was, I couldn't even speak properly.

"Well, Penny *is* a small pony," said Dad matter-of-factly. For a moment it was quiet around the table. Cecilie looked up from a magazine she was reading and peered at us, oddly. Even she, who was totally uninterested in animals, realized that this was some sort of milestone for me, and smiled sympathetically at me. I wasn't even able to smile back.

"Julia, you've grown three inches in half a year! No wonder you notice a difference with regards to Penny," said Mom suddenly. With revulsion, I thought about the measurement we did half an hour earlier, when Dad quietly stated that I was now 5 feet 3 inches tall. *Over 15 inches higher than my pony!* I thought. *That's not going to work...*

"Would it..." I swallowed, trying to gather up courage. My parents looked quizzically at me. I avoided their eyes until after I had asked the question.

"Is there a chance that I could have both Penny and... another horse?"

My mom looked as if she had been struck by lightning. Before she had a chance to say anything, I quickly added some arguments, but even I could hear how completely unreasonable and desperate they sounded.

"You know, it wouldn't be twice as expensive! I wouldn't be taking riding lessons with Penny, and I wouldn't need any new tack or anything for her either. Maybe we could even have her on outside boarding only. That's probably much cheaper," I pondered out loud.

"Julia! Come to your senses, will you?" interrupted Dad in a sharp tone of voice. I felt my hope sink, and the heavy, unpleasant feeling from earlier in the day came back.

"First of all, it's way too expensive for us to have *two* horses! I can't believe you would even suggest such a thing! It's more than expensive enough with one, even if the upkeep of a second horse would be cheaper." My Dad looked me firmly in the eye, but kept his voice calm. "Secondly, there is the issue of time. You'll be starting ninth grade now, and you've said yourself that there'll be more homework and longer days with every year from now on…"

"That's right! We wouldn't see you at all anymore, if you were going to be at the stable all day, taking care of two horses. It would simply be too much work!" This time it was Mom who looked sternly at me.

"And last but not least, Julia, Penny is only twelve years old, right?" started Dad, in a gentler voice now. I nodded slowly, and had a pretty good idea what he was going to say.

"From what I understand, she's pretty good at both dressage and jumping, she's very sound and enjoys being ridden. It wouldn't be a very nice thing to do to her, to practically retire her this early in her life. You see that too, don't you, sweetheart?"

I nodded again, staring at the table. That was part of the problem; I agreed completely!

"If only it was possible to make her bigger," I said quietly and gave a long sigh. Mom looked sympathetically at me.

"Just think about it for a while. You don't have to make a decision right now. But I assume the options are to either keep Penny and ride her very carefully, or to sell her and buy a bigger horse with the money. We'll let you do that, and we'll continue to pay for most of the expenses as we've been doing."

I shook my head, feeling tears in my eyes again.

"I'll just keep Penny then," I muttered, but stopped short of actually saying the rest of what I was thinking, which was *I don't want any other horse!* That would have been a little too cliché, I thought. Then I went into my bedroom to have a good cry.

Chapter 9

The next day I woke up early. When I opened my eyes, I looked at the clock; 7:50 a.m. With a smile I noted that I could still stay in bed for a couple of hours, but when I wasn't able to go back to sleep for fifteen minutes so I decided to get up anyway. *This way Penny won't have to get so hot carrying me around,* I reflected sadly as I went into the bathroom. It was a sunny day, and I had a feeling it was going to get pretty steamy later.

While I biked down the dirt road on my way to the stable, I reflected on how wonderful it actually felt to be out early in the morning, once I managed to get out of bed. It was almost eight thirty, the morning sun felt warm on my face, the birds were chirping and the sky was blue, without a cloud in sight. I forced myself to enjoy it, something that wasn't really difficult, and pushed the Penny issue out of my mind for a while. Upon my arrival, I locked my bike to the usual tree and went into the stable to get the halter.

"Hey sweetie, what are you doing here?" I said quietly to Nikita, who was standing in her stall. She pushed her muzzle gently toward the bars, as if to say something. I looked at her stall neighbors, Silver and Bonny, who were also looking at me curiously inside the quiet, semi-dark stable. Silver was a dapple New Forest pony, very cute, and Bonny was a chocolate brown Welsh pony. I didn't really know much about these horses, except that Silver was getting on in years and mainly functioned as a recreational riding horse for its new, young owner, and Bonny was competing in the small jumping classes with its young owner.

"You poor things, why are you inside on a nice day like this?" I asked in a low voice, even though I knew they were fine. I knew they would be taken outside in the gravel paddock at two o'clock, and would stay outside until at least eight o'clock. And they got plenty of good hay three times a day. That's how life was around here for the horses that didn't go to a summer pasture.

Both Silver and Bonny quickly lost interest in me, and continued eating their hay, but Nikita kept staring at me, and sniffed curiously at my hand when I held it up to her. I raised my other hand too, but that made her jumpy.

"I'm sorry, girl. Martine has made you all nervous, hasn't she?" I whispered. I wanted to go in to her, but I knew that you're not supposed to go in to someone else's horse without their permission. So I stayed out, but kept an eye on Nikita for a while. She started eating her hay, but continued to look at me every so often. Sometimes her head would pop up, her ears pointed, and she would stop chewing and stare, as if she heard something interesting. She had a noble head, and was tall and slender. Probably a large 14.1 hands high pony, about 57 inches, was my guess.

After a few minutes I said goodbye to the three ponies and went in to get Penny's halter and grooming box, which I then left at the tethering post. I was surprised to see that there was somebody training in the arena already. *Wow! Somebody came early today,* I thought. I walked toward the arena, and when I got closer, I saw it was Linn. I should have known. I heard the day before that Linn would be taking care of the horses by herself for a while, because Anette was on vacation.

They were trotting around a longe line, and the horse went willingly and soon walked nicely, though not exactly with the greatest collection I'd ever seen. The horse, whose name was Proud Misty, was a large, five-year-old bay horse, and Linn had told me that he was imported from Denmark. He'd been with her for about two years now, and a few weeks ago they placed first – against some pretty stiff competition – in a low-level class at an event on the south coast. After that she had started training him toward a medium level. I knew that her other horse, a bay mare named Marina, was in the high medium-level classes, but since Linn focused more on teaching and running the riding center, she didn't have much time for racing.

Linn was very focused as she worked, so it took a few minutes before she noticed me. When she did, she slackened the reins and steered the gelding toward me.

"Hi there, Julia! So, you're back from Spain, you lucky girl!" Linn said with a big smile.

"Hi, Linn! Yes, we got back yesterday. And it's wonderful to be back again!" I answered, smiling. Linn halted, almost without touching the reins, and stroked her horse on the neck a couple of times before she turned to me again.

"Well, nothing much has happened around here," she said, thoughtfully. "You already know that I did some eventing this summer, just at the low level, with this guy, and yes, we started in another one as well while you were gone." She looked at me, secretively.

"So – how did it go?" I asked excitedly.

"Well, first of all, we made our debut at the intermediate level!" she said proudly. I applauded her, humorously.

"We placed fourth, out of twenty riders," she told me. I congratulated her, and was genuinely happy for her. Linn was a very good, considerate rider who trained her horses conscientiously. I gave her a brief recount of my vacation and then, with some hesitation, I gathered up courage and asked, "Um... I noticed that two of the paddocks are empty right now," I started, and Linn nodded. "Couldn't the horses who are in the stable use them?" I asked as innocently as I could.

"You're thinking about those three ponies in Stable B?" asked Linn, sounding a little short. I worried that it might have been rude of me to ask. After all, it was none of my business.

"Believe me, I'd be more than happy to put them outside." The way Linn said it, I understood that it wasn't me she was mad at.

"The problem is that Martine wants Nikita to be inside when she arrives, and she always comes later in the morning. But because Nikita gets so nervous when she's left inside alone, Martine has somehow managed to talk the owners of those other two ponies into making their horses stay inside too," Linn said. We both rolled our eyes a little, but dropped the issue after that.

"But, Julia, there's something else ..." This time Linn was the one who hesitated and looked unsure. I looked questioningly at her.

"I don't mean to butt in or anything, but how are things going with you and Penny now? I mean, I happened to see you riding her yesterday, and I thought... Well, I thought it looked like you've grown a lot this summer, if you know what I mean." Linn looked at me with a wrinkle between her eyebrows after her obvious hint about the very issue I had been worried about for the past day. I glared angrily at the ground, and just shrugged my shoulders.

"As I said, I don't want to butt in, but I have to be honest, and I'm afraid it's time for you to start thinking seriously about what you're going to do with Penny," she said firmly.

I remained stiff and continued to stare at the ground. It made me feel childish that I couldn't answer her properly, but I simply wasn't able to pull myself together. Why did Linn have to start poking at this sensitive issue, which was so new and difficult for me?

"Well, I'd better get back to riding before Misty cools off," she said finally. The gelding was resting on one leg with his eyes semi-closed, but as soon as Linn straightened up and gently picked up the reins he raised his head, alert and ready to go again. I watched them as they walked away. Linn's long legs were well above the horse's girth area, even with long dressage stirrups.

I walked into the pasture with heavy steps, then collapsed in the grass and dissolved into tears. I seemed to have turned into a regular crying machine lately. You could just push a button and the tears flowed freely.

After a while I saw Penny out of the corner of my eye, walking toward me. She sniffed my neck and nudged me gently, as if she was asking what I was crying about. Still sobbing, I stroked her neck, but a small gasp of laughter snuck into the crying when I got up. I was so much taller than she was! I could easily stand on one side of her and stroke her shoulder on the other side, and I had to bend down to cuddle her head. This really was pretty hopeless, I suddenly realized. I knew that I most likely wouldn't get a whole lot taller over the next few years, because I was already almost the same height as my mom, and my dad was not very tall either.

"If only you were 8 inches higher, then we wouldn't have this problem! Then I could've kept you for as long as you live," I whispered to Penny. She answered with a snort, as if she took offense and was saying that she was perfectly happy being the way she was.

"I guess I could just keep you," I said next, "but then I would have to give up riding!"

"Besides, it wouldn't be a nice thing to do to Penny." Dad's comment was still stuck in my mind.

Then I thought about yesterday's trail ride. We had ridden up the usual trail, and I noticed that Penny was in abnormally bad shape. We had kept to walking and trotting, and only rode for half an hour. But it hadn't been a very good ride, because it was really hot, with swarms of insects, and Penny was sweating and snorting and clearly showing that she'd rather be back in her pasture. I hoped things would be better this morning, and glanced at my watch. It was already nine fifteen, so I decided to hurry and get the most out of the hour before it got hotter. I threaded the halter over Penny's head and led her with me. The other ponies were grazing, and even Prisci only looked up briefly as we passed before she continued eating.

I was still in the same low spirits and totally absorbed by my own thoughts as I stood in the farmyard brushing Penny, so I jumped when somebody suddenly tapped me on the shoulder.

"Eline! Hi," I said in surprise. She's not known to make contact with others very easily.

"Hi," she said, looking a little unsure. "I was wondering if you'd like to go for a ride with Chestnut and me?"

Chapter 10

I won't deny that I was baffled! Eline, with her expensive stallion. Eline, who always rode alone. Eline, who was always so short and unfriendly... *She* had just asked *me* to go riding with her! True, I had experienced a lighter side of her during the mare's visit right before I left for my vacation, but I was still very surprised.

"Sure!" I answered, forcing a smile. She nodded once, and went into the stable. Had it been any other time before my vacation, I would probably have burst out laughing, especially if Pia had been around. But at the moment I didn't think it was funny at all. To be honest, I was slightly irritated for a few seconds, because I kind of wanted to ride alone right now. I wasn't in the mood for company, to act all friendly to a lady who had barely even talked to me in the past, and who happened to be riding a beautiful horse that fit her perfectly. *Take it easy, Julia,* I told myself sternly. *Maybe Eline isn't the type you have to act all cheerful for.*

The saddle and bridle were on, and I was just fastening tendon boots on Penny when Eline emerged from Stable A with Chestnut on a lead rope. The stallion looked great, as always. He stopped at the mounting ramp, and stood completely still, with ears pointed while Eline got up. She started him in a walk and came riding toward me with a smile on her face.

"Not exactly how things were a year ago! Do you remember?" she asked. I nodded.

"Oh yes, I remember how he used to bounce around in the beginning. You've done a great job with him," I commented, tightening the cinch and getting into the saddle.

Eline thanked me for the compliment and smiled.

"Do you want to ride up the hill and through the woods over there?" I asked, even though I was already on my way. She gave a nod of agreement and let Chestnut follow Penny. We rode up to the hill and got out on a gravel road after a short distance through the woods. I felt the need to start a conversation, and was actually a little curious about these two who were doing so well together.

"How is he around other horses?" I asked, only because it was the first thing that came to mind.

"Pretty good, actually. I rode with Linda and Coliseum a few days ago, and it went just fine. Of course, we were only walking and trotting, and I got to ride in front the whole time, so it wasn't exactly the biggest challenge. But I've been very deliberate about training him around others in the arena, to get him used to having other horses around without getting all uptight about it. But of course it's different when you ride in a line, since that triggers a certain degree of rivalry," she continued.

I drove Penny on to make her keep up with Chestnut's

long stride, and my face broke into a genuinely big smile. That was the most I'd ever heard Eline say all at once!

"You're probably right," I added, and went on to suggest that we start trotting. Eline drove her stallion into a calm, balanced trot, and he quickly collected himself into a fairly free form. I noticed that Penny was more excited today than yesterday, and the reason was probably a combination of us riding with another horse, plus it wasn't as hot today.

After riding lightly for a while, I seated myself deeper in the saddle and tried to get Penny into a more collected form. She responded willingly, placed her hind legs more underneath, and relaxed her back as well as her neck. After this, her trot got more comfortable since she was making bigger steps with more resilience, and she felt nice and soft. I smiled with pride over my pony. It wasn't always this easy to get her to walk so collectedly.

"How nicely she walks! You're both very skilled," commented Eline after having watched us for a while. I smiled with pride.

"She doesn't always walk this well," I said almost apologetically. "Maybe she's trying harder because of Chestnut," I added.

After awhile I used my seat to put the brakes on, barely using the reins. Penny immediately slowed down to a walk, and just as she started relaxing, I gave more reins and let her stretch her neck properly. Eline did the same. We continued walking in silence, until I thought of asking how things were going with Cissi, the mare who was covered by Chestnut.

"It went really well! They were together for three whole days, and seemed to have a great time. No signs of any kicking or biting. Actually, they behaved like a couple of love birds," said Eline, and I almost thought I saw stars sparkling in her eyes.

"Were they together the whole time, both day and night?" I wondered.

"No, we took them inside at night. Since there was space available in Stable A, it wasn't a problem. Chestnut has a tendency to gain weight really easily, so I prefer to keep him inside at night if he goes outside during the day and eats all that high-energy grass. And of course Tom wanted his princess to be safely locked up in a stall at night, especially since she was staying in an unfamiliar place," she explained. Once again I was taken by surprise at her being so talkative all of a sudden.

"Yeah, I'm sure it's good to keep things under control," I commented. She nodded, and then asked if we should try galloping a little as we approached a slight uphill stretch. I agreed, somewhat hesitantly. We picked up the reins and made contact with the horses before starting a slow canter. Chestnut looked as if he just wanted to speed things up, but Eline sat deeply in the saddle and tried to make him use his energy for a nice collected pace rather than for speed. She eventually succeeded, at least for a few yards, to get him to almost sit on his hind legs and walk in a beautiful, high form.

I let Penny walk as she pleased, but after a short distance she started breathing heavily and walking slower. With a frown, I drove her forward. Then I noticed that Chestnut was also breathing heavily, and so we both slowed down and let the horses walk on long reins. Chestnut shook his head and snorted from the effort.

"Wow, that was fun!" exclaimed Eline, stroking her horse proudly on the neck. "I don't think we've ever managed a more collected form than that! It must be because of what you mentioned earlier, that he's kind of showing off to Penny, plus the nice road and fresh air. But as you saw, he got worn out pretty quickly, so I don't think he's got the muscle to carry himself like that for very long," said Eline, her eyes beaming.

"He was amazing! That was just as good as what Linn and Marina might do when they're at their best! Actually, I'm not even sure that I've seen anything quite that good from them!" I said, because I was really very impressed. Eline smiled, a little indulgent, I noticed, as if the praise from a 14-year-old didn't mean much. It irritated me a little, and I fell silent.

"But...um, am I wrong, or did Penny get a little worn out too?"

"Yes," I said. "She hasn't been ridden in three weeks, so she's in pretty bad shape. I've been on vacation, and my exercise rider is gone now too, so I have to train her again," I explained. Eline nodded slowly.

"Linn told me she's going to do a small dressage event at the stable in a month or so, at the end of August. Would you be interested in signing up for that?" Eline looked at me in a friendly and quizzical way. Once again I was surprised at how friendly and outgoing she was, and wondered why she usually hid behind such a boring side of herself at the stable. For a moment I forgot my problems and felt excited at the thought of eventing.

"Oh, that sounds great!" I said with a smile. "Dressage is a lot of fun, and Penny and I have started getting things together now," I added happily as I bent down over my little pony and gave her a hug. Inside I suddenly felt a jolt though. I knew it wouldn't be a good idea to push Penny with hard-core training for an event, and to ride a demanding dressage program the way things were right now. I sat up straight and swallowed heavily. Stiffly, I stared at Penny's neck, and started cleaning her mane.

"Is everything all right, Julia?" Eline asked quietly.

"I... no, it's not." Before I knew it, I blurted out my problem: "I've grown too big for Penny!"

Eline didn't look surprised, but encouraged me to continue.

"You only have to look at us to know, of course, and I notice it myself too. It's not much fun to ride her when she gets tired so quickly, and it's all because of my size. But I don't know if I should sell her, or what I should do!" I exclaimed, shrugging my shoulders and sighing heavily. "After all, I've had her for four years now, and we've had so much fun together! I've learned a lot from her, and I love her so much!" I continued.

"Yes, I understand how difficult the situation must be for you," said Eline sympathetically. "Actually, I went through something similar myself many years ago."

I looked questioningly at her, but she seemed to be lost in thought. Then she started telling me her story.

"I'll never forget my first pony. It was a Shetland

86

pony, a really tough stallion, actually. He was the one who taught me all the basics of riding, the balance and the aids. Well, with good help from my father, that is. Oh, I had so much fun with him. Mini Black was his name. We eventually competed in pony gallops and small show jumping events, and did a lot of fun-filled trail rides out in the woods. He was so sure-footed! But when I was..." Eline paused while trying to remember. "I think I was almost twelve when people started looking at us a little funny while I was riding him, and I overheard some comments. I was very hurt by it, and finally I asked my dad what he thought. He told me straight out that I had gotten too tall for the pony, but because he was a strong Shetland pony at his best age, and I was very thin, he didn't have any problems carrying me. The problem was that we couldn't jump anymore, because when we did, I knocked down the hurdles with my legs, and he couldn't run as fast as before with me hanging and dangling!" Eline fell silent and looked at me. I nodded, because I knew exactly what she was talking about.

"I... I..." I stuttered, but couldn't really think of anything sensible to say. Quietly, I led us down a shortcut, which would take us back to the stable in only twenty minutes at a walk, because we had already been gone for almost forty-five minutes.

Finally I couldn't stop myself from asking, "What did you do with Mini Black?"

"I sold him to a good riding school and bought a strong cold-blooded mare. It took me awhile, but of course I realized that I just couldn't keep him any longer.

He was only ten years old at the time and had many more good years ahead of him, during which he would be able to remain active. In fact, I didn't regret it for a moment. Of course I *missed* him, but I didn't ever wish that I hadn't sold him. Besides, my new horse, Freia, needed so much of my time and love and training, that it didn't take long before I thoroughly enjoyed riding again, and this time without a guilty conscience," Eline finished.

After the ride I stood around just thinking. I had showered Penny and dried her off with a sweat scraper. Now I leaned toward her while she was grazing. I clicked my tongue and led her into the pasture. She was almost completely dry, and I watched her briefly and then jumped up on her back. In fact, all I had to do was throw my leg over her back, and there I was. I hugged her tightly, and lay down on her while thinking.

Sure, I'd read books about it, heard about it, and even seen it, but I hadn't ever allowed the thought to sink in. *One day you will be too big for your dear, sweet pony, and then you have, unless you happen to have a horse ranch or a lot of money*, as my mom said, *two choices: Quit riding the way you normally would, or sell the pony and buy a new horse.*

That is the cold, hard truth, I thought dismally.

I loosened the rope so that Penny could move more freely while she was grazing, and we wandered around like that, enjoying the summer sun. Maybe this was our last summer together...

Chapter 11

"Make sure your outer shoulder doesn't fall out too far! Use the reins against the neck! That's good. Keep her there," said Linn, who was standing in the middle of the track in the dressage arena. Penny and I were having a half-hour private lesson with her, and we were both very warm and fully focused. Just now we were practicing traverse in trot, an exercise that we just recently started getting better at, and Penny was doing very well. She walked collected and relaxed to the reins, her legs in the right position, nicely bent and stepping correctly.

"Very good! Stop when you get to the M, then ride lightly," Linn said. I straightened myself in the saddle, positioned Penny a little back and laid the outer leg aid slightly forward again, the way it looks when you ride straight forward. Linn had us trot a lap around the track before she asked me to halt next to her.

"You guys are doing great!" she praised, and scratched Penny behind the ears. I slackened the reins and Penny stood for a few seconds in the same collected form before she stretched her neck and shook her head.

"So you've decided to sell her?" asked Linn suddenly, giving me a serious look. I nodded slowly.

"I've thought about it while riding her this week, ever since I got back from Spain, and I think it'll be best for both her and me. At least for her," I added quietly.

"The best for both of you," Linn corrected firmly. "You're doing the right thing by selling her. I've been seeing it for a long time, and now I'm telling it to you straight. You have great potential in dressage, Julia. You're calm and have fine, but clear aids, and you have a talent for making the horse relax," Linn praised.

I blushed at all this unexpected praise, but it also made me feel warm and happy inside. I thanked her appreciatively. Actually, I had always been more interested in jumping, because of the speed and the excitement. But over the last few months, I had come to like dressage more and more, and realized what incredible fun it could be when you managed to do things correctly.

"It's nothing but the truth! In my opinion, what you need is a large pony who is sensitive, has a fluid stride and the capacity for difficult exercises, because with a pony like that, you can do really well," said Linn. I looked at her with surprise.

"But I was kind of thinking of getting a small… horse," I said slowly.

"Well… since you can compete in the pony class through your sixteenth birthday, you still have two and a half years left as a pony rider! And if you find it difficult to part with your new pony at that point, you can also compete in the horse classes after that, as long as the pony is at least 14.1 hands high. I would definitely recommend that you get a pony," stated Linn. I decided to consider her advice, thanked her for the lesson and rode back to the stable.

It was ten in the morning, and Penny and I had just had our very last riding lesson together! As I said, I had thought about it for a whole week and I noticed how heavy Penny's breathing was when I rode her. Especially during galloping, and when I couldn't even use leg aids, I knew the answer to my difficult dilemma. Linn's comments about my potential helped too, I won't deny it. *I'll start working on an ad when I get home,* I thought as I sighed. At the same time I felt a hard knot in my stomach. Then I leaned forward and whispered into Penny's ear, "We still have a month left of summer vacation, and if I'm going to sell you, I'll at least make sure that you go to a very good home!" Penny looked at me and snorted contentedly.

Just as I rode out of the arena, Martine and Nikita rode in. When I smiled at her, she actually smiled back. I couldn't help but admire Nikita as she walked by. Her ears were pointed, and she looked interestedly at Penny as we passed each other. She was a beautiful bay, completely brown with a long, black mane and tail, and a really cute white collar by her muzzle. I sighed with apprehension when I saw all the tack she had on, however, and halted. Nikita had an extra device on the lower noseband, which was very tight, and the idiotic elastic martingale that

Martine had put on her, way too tightly, was preventing her from raising her head at all.

As for Martine, she was wearing spurs and carrying a whip, and I knew that inside Nikita's mouth was a sharp bit. Martine let Nikita walk on the square track, but with tight rains the whole way, and even from where I was, I could tell that the pony was all tensed up. After only one round, she started trying to avoid the bit and raise her head, but all the tack prevented it, so she walked with her tongue out of her mouth as she started thrashing her head frantically.

I was so saddened by just looking at her, and was about to continue riding when Martine suddenly yelled, "She's always acting up in the arena. She's just pushing her limits with me."

I shook my head without answering, and walked away with Penny.

Outside the stable were Bonny, Silver, and Angie – one of the Arabians in Stable A – all saddled up next to their owners, who were busy tightening girths and fixing stirrups. Angie was a cute, dappled filly, and her adult owner, who also owned the other Arabian at the stable, was a very nice lady.

"Hi!" I said with a smile, and dismounted Penny. "Going for a trail ride?" I asked. Angie's owner walked toward me looking cheerful.

"The two girls asked so nicely," she started saying. "Their parents won't let them ride out alone yet – which is perfectly understandable. One of them is only nine! So they have to ride with somebody older than they are. And apparently they find it very stressful to ride with Martine, because she always wants to run and mess around the whole time. So they asked me to take a short trail ride with them instead," she said. By the expression on her face, I could tell that she didn't mind at all, and was happy to go with the two girls. Most of the people at the stable were familiar with the way Martine rode.

"I don't blame them," I said sympathetically. "It's nice of you to take them! Have a good one!" I said, and led Penny into the stable. From outside, I could hear, "Are you ready? Here we go!"

I smiled as I pulled the saddle off of my little black pony, took the bridle off and put on a halter. Then I rinsed her off in the washroom. Penny showed her teeth and was clearly enjoying the shower. She drank eagerly as I held the hose up for her. I scraped off most of the water with a sweat scraper before leading her outside and I let her graze while I sat down to enjoy the sun. To my surprise I found that the whole issue of selling Penny actually felt a little easier with every passing day. Also, I couldn't help but notice a feeling of excitement and joy at the prospect of getting a new, larger pony.

From where I was sitting, I could see the dressage arena clearly, and almost shuddered at what I saw. Martine and Nikita were riding a trot, the mare tenser than ever, but the tight martingale forced her to be in an unnatural position. Martine hardly ever used her leg aids, only the spurs, to drive her horse forward, and from a fast, unbalanced trot they went into a stiff and choppy gallop. Nikita was clearly leaning inward while her head was turned outward, and as I watched them it was hard to believe that this was actually a horse owner riding her own horse in this way. It looked more like a beginner trying to ride a difficult pony for the first time.

"I don't understand what she's doing!" exclaimed somebody a short distance away from me. I turned to see Michelle with Redrose and Heidi with her horse, Gollum. They were both staring in the direction of the riding arena, shaking their heads. I felt my spirits perk up and walked over to join them.

"What do you think about her riding?" I asked curiously, and they immediately knew what I was referring to.

"It's downright reprehensible!" said Heidi, a little precocious, in view of the fact that she was only seventeen.

"Her riding is so bad... it's unbelievable!" said Michelle, a worrisome wrinkle forming on her forehead. I nodded in agreement.

"I've ridden Nikita myself. I got to ride her one of the first days after she came here, and she was absolutely fantastic. *Very* responsive to aids and eager to please, even with very little tack on," said Heidi. Michelle and I nodded.

"You know what Martine said to me a little while ago, when she rode into the arena?" I asked, and continued without waiting for an answer. "She said that Nikita is always acting up in the arena and is just pushing her limits!"

Heidi looked as if she was about to blow a fuse, then

she jumped on her horse as she said firmly, "I think we've seen enough of this! There is no doubt that she's ruining that wonderful pony. I'm going over there and telling her what I think."

With that she rode off, and Michelle got up on Redrose and followed. "This, I don't want to miss," she said, winking humorously at me.

I hurried inside to get some energy feed for Penny, and then gave it to her outside while I kept an eye on what was happening in the arena. Heidi stopped Gollum in front of Martine and Nikita, who started stepping nervously. Redrose stood a little further back and rested, but it was clear that Michelle was listening to the discussion. It wasn't possible for me to hear what anybody was saying, but I saw that Heidi made some big movements on horseback, while Martine watched her angrily. At the same moment, Linn emerged from Stable A, leading Marina, and I quietly called her over to me.

By now, the two in the arena were shouting at each other so loudly that even those of us standing by the stable could clearly hear their voices. Gollum raised his head up high, wondering what was going on. Nikita looked like she was about to explode, but suddenly Martine made a violent movement, and pushed her spurs hard into Nikita's sides. The mare reared up, and then galloped out of the arena! For a moment it looked like Nikita had run away, but as she came racing toward us at full speed I saw Martine leaning over the pony's neck, driving her to go faster! The horse's neck was soaked with sweat from having run around the arena several times, and we could see the whites of her eyes and her ears stuck flat to her neck. When they passed us it looked as if Nikita hesitated for a moment and glanced at us, but Martine didn't seem to see us at all. She just yelled "Yah!" and slammed her spurs into the pony's sides! Together they stormed down the gravel road from the stable and continued uphill toward the jumping arena.

Linn and I glanced at each other, and I'd never seen her so shocked before. Her eyes were wide and her mouth partially open, but she controlled herself in order to soothe Marina, who was pretty upset that somebody had just galloped past the tip of her nose. Even Penny reared up, so I had my hands full trying to control her for a few minutes while Heidi and Michelle came trotting toward us, looking just as shocked as we were.

"What the..." Linn interrupted herself while trying to prevent Marina from rearing. "What the heck was *that* all about?" she finally yelled.

"Would you like me to go and get her?" asked Heidi at the same time, missing Linn's question. Linn thought about it for a few seconds, and then shook her head. Just then Eline and Chestnut walked up the gravel road, and she looked shaken and had a questioning expression on her face.

"Eline!" called Linn, relieved. "Would you go and try to get Martine back here, please? I'm afraid she might hurt both herself and the horse!" Eline had already turned Chestnut around and kicked him into a gallop even before Linn was done talking, so she must have gotten the point.

"Please dismount from your horses, I'm just going

to turn this one out first," Linn said firmly, and led the agitated horse toward one of the paddocks. I jumped up on Penny, trotted her up to the pasture and let her go inside with her friends before I ran quickly back down to the farmyard.

"Now, let me hear the whole story," said Linn, looking primarily at Heidi. "All I saw was that you and Martine were having a rather spirited... discussion, out there in the arena, and then suddenly started shouting and screaming. And then Martine and Nikita came flying past us like a hurricane."

"Well, you see, we... the three of us," Heidi said, catching Michelle's and my eyes to include us, "were watching Martine riding that poor Nikita really badly in the arena. I rode Nikita myself a year ago, and I know that she needs sensitive treatment, and then she'll go like a cannon. So we were all pretty irritated as we watched what Martine was doing. We think it's gone too far, the way that girl treats her horse," said Heidi passionately, looking anxiously at Linn.

Linn didn't make any comment, but just asked, "So what did you do?"

Heidi shrugged her shoulders. "Well, Michelle and I rode over to the arena. We were going there to train anyway, and then I shouted to Martine. I asked her why she was using her spurs so hard and why she kept jerking at her horse's mouth. That was enough to make her scream at me that it was none of my business, and that I knew nothing about her horse, and so on. So I yelled back the same thing I told you guys, that Nikita is a sensitive pony that should be treated with respect and that what she was doing was bordering on cruelty to animals. That's when she totally flipped. She told me to shut up and get away from her, and then she kicked the spurs into Nikita and took off!" finished Heidi. She looked, if possible, even more upset than a few moments ago.

With a grave look on her face, Linn glanced at each of us in turn. Michelle gave a confirming nod, and I said calmly, "Heidi is right."

"Totally unacceptable," mumbled Linn suddenly. Then she left us and went into her office, which was a room connected to Stable A. We watched her with a questioning look on our faces. Suddenly Gollum broke the tension by scraping intensely and impatiently at the ground with his hoof. Heidi turned to Michelle.

"How about a trail ride instead? I don't think I could handle any training right now. I'm too stressed out," she said.

"Same here," answered Michelle. "Thanks to that stupid girl. Her pony deserves a nicer and better owner," she said. The two girls mounted their horses and rode away as they waved to me with a resigned smile. I felt so sad.

Chapter 12

"Julia, I have an idea!" Mom yelled the moment I walked into the hallway at home. I took off my chaps and riding boots and went out on the deck, where Mom was sitting with sunglasses, a magazine and a cold drink.

"Oh, you do, huh?" I said with a smile, and then sat down on a patio chair.

"What about selling Penny to Fredrik?" Mom looked at me with such excitement, you'd think she had just offered me three beautiful horses. I hesitated for a moment. Fredrik was my exercise rider, who was usually responsible for Penny twice a week, and whenever I was unavailable. He and I were the same age, and he had definitely contributed to getting Penny to her current level, because he was very good at dressage.

"That may not be a bad idea," I said, still thinking.

"He'd probably continue to board her at Linn's Stable, and that way you could still see her almost every day. You may even be able to go riding with him and Penny, on your new horse!" Mom said, sounding very excited. I stared at her, and slowly my face broke into a big smile.

"He is pretty thin and not very tall, so he's a good size for Penny," I added enthusiastically. "I'll go call him now! He should be back from vacation by now, because he has Penny tomorrow." Mom nodded encouragingly.

I jumped up from the chair and went into the family room to get the phone. It had been awhile since I had talked to him, because most of our communication about Penny happened through text messaging. Therefore, I was surprised to hear the low voice that said, "hello."

"Hi, it's Julia!" I said cheerfully.

"Oh, hi, Julia! I was actually going to call *you*," he answered, in a cheerful voice. We chatted briefly about our vacations, and then I asked if he remembered that he had Penny the next day.

"Yes," he said. "But, I was wondering if you could come over to the stable while I'm there tomorrow?"

"Oh, yeah? Why? When will you be there?" I asked, a little curious.

"There's something I need to talk to you about," he said, sounding serious now. "I'll be there at about seven o'clock. Could you meet me then? In the evening, that is," he added teasingly.

"All right. I'll see you then. Take care!" I said, and hung up, a little puzzled. Why did he want to see me? Had something happened to him? What did he need to talk to me about? The questions were buzzing in my head, and suddenly I remembered that I hadn't even gotten to say what I had called him about! *Oh well, there will be more then one serious thing to discuss tomorrow then,* I thought with a sigh.

"Julia, what's the matter?" Sara asked with a worried look on her face. Sara was my best friend at school, and at the moment she and I and a couple of other girls from school were at the beach swimming. We had already been talking for about an hour, telling each other all about our vacations, but after a while I had become distracted and wasn't really participating in the conversation any more, because... that's right... I was thinking about Penny. When Sara asked, I told her about my decision to sell my pony, and how I felt about it.

"Ohhh, I'm so sorry," she said sympathetically and hugged me. "I don't know what I'd do if we had to sell Basse!" She raised her eyebrows and shook her head. Basse is Sara's lively, black lab. Even my two other friends, Marie and Thea, who normally rolled their eyes whenever I mentioned the word "horse," tried to comfort me. They were sitting next to me on the sand, and seemed to understand why I wasn't in the best of moods.

"Hey girls, maybe we can lift Julia's spirits by going for a swim!" said Marie suddenly with a humorous spark in her eyes. She grabbed the water toy she had brought, an enormous, inflatable crocodile that she bought on her vacation in Greece, and ran toward the water. The rest of us smiled at each other and then followed her. We dove into the water, which got deeper only a few yards out, and started splashing and teasing each other. Then we had a play fight, getting on top of the crocodile and taking turns pulling each other off of it. We were having a great time. I actually managed to forget about Penny for a while, and my mood improved significantly.

A few hours later, I was back on my bike again, this time on my way to the stable. I was anxious to find out what Fredrik wanted to talk about. He had sounded so serious on the phone the day before, so I doubted that it was anything particularly pleasant. I locked my bike at the usual place and walked up to the stable. On the way, I passed the paddock where Nikita was standing, together with Bonny and Silver. It was unusual for me to see her outside, but then I remembered that I normally went to the stable early in the morning, and that Nikita gets to go outside in the afternoon and evening.

I shuddered as I thought about yesterday, when Martine had lost it. Eline and Chestnut had returned about twenty minutes later, with a humbler looking Martine and a sweaty and jumpy Nikita in tow. Neither of them said anything while I was there, but I wondered what Eline had said to get that crazy girl to come back with her to the stable. I went home a little while later.

Now I stopped at the paddock and looked at the brown mare. She was covered in dried mud, which made me wonder if Martine had ridden her today. I could easily imagine that Martine had just left Nikita in the hot sun yesterday, without rinsing her off first. There wasn't much shade in this paddock, and no grass, so it must have been pretty hot for Nikita.

Calmly, I reached out my hand and called her. Nikita looked straight at me and did not look away, but she didn't move. After a few minutes, both Silver and Bonny walked slowly toward me, but when they realized I didn't have any treats, they padded away again, sniffing around

for bits of hay that they might have missed after their dinner. I stood completely still by the fence, and finally, after quite a while, Nikita took a few uncertain steps toward me. Eventually she was only a couple of yards away, sniffing curiously at my hand. I rummaged through my pockets, and found a little piece of carrot, which I reached out to her. She took it hesitantly and looked at me with her beautiful, almond-shaped eyes while she chewed.

"You are so beautiful, do you know that?" I said quietly and soothingly, stroking my hand lightly over her muzzle. She let me do it, but I could tell that she had tensed up while I was petting her. "If I was your owner, I would never use spurs on you, or all that silly tack that Martine uses either," I told her. "And I definitely wouldn't ride you the way she does!" I added firmly. Nikita raised her head and pointed her ears as she looked over toward the farmyard in front of Stable B. I turned and saw Penny who was walking next to Fredrik.

"Bye, sweetie! I'll see you soon," I whispered to Nikita. Then I jogged over to my pony.

"Hi, Fredrik! What...?" I exclaimed and stopped. Since Fredrik and I are usually at the stable on different days, it had been over two months since I had seen him, and the change in his appearance was a total shock.

"Hi!" he said. "I know, I thought you might see the problem for yourself," he said, stroking Penny on the neck. I knew perfectly well what he meant. Fredrik was now even taller than I was!

Chapter 13

"So what do we do now?" asked Fredrik with sadness in his voice. We were sitting in the grass near the stables, while Penny grazed peacefully next to us.

"Well, actually I wanted to talk to you because... because I've decided to sell Penny, since I've grown too big for her too," I began. Fredrik looked at me knowingly, understanding what a difficult step this had to be for me.

"And I wanted to talk to *you* because I realized that I was too big to ride Penny, and needed to cancel the exercise rider agreement that we have," he said. We sat silently for a while, just admiring the beautiful little pony that had meant so much to both of us. I don't think I was the only one who was getting choked up, because when I started speaking it took a while before Fredrik turned toward me again.

"But would you be interested in continuing as my exercise rider after I get a new horse? I'll probably get a 14 hands high pony, and it shouldn't take too long," I said eagerly. To my surprise I noticed that Fredrik hesitated.

"Of course you'll get to try it out before you decide, several times if you want, and there's no obligation involved. It's just that it's hard to find a good exercise rider, and I've been very happy with you," I said as I smiled at him. Stroking a hand through his blonde hair, he gave me a quick smile back.

"Julia, I wouldn't mind continuing with you, you know that," he said in a serious voice, and then suddenly looked me in the eyes. I got kind of embarrassed and looked at the ground.

"But the thing is... Well, I'm really more interested in jumping. I've been doing dressage for a long time now, and don't really think I'm getting anywhere. And since I know that you prefer that I train dressage, I..."

"No, no, Fredrik!" I burst out. He gave me a surprised look. "This is perfect!" I continued. "You see, both Linn and I are thinking that I should be focusing more on dressage... that I might actually have some potential in that direction. So I won't be doing much jumping anymore. But it would be great if you could do it! That way the pony would get a little variation!" I said happily. Fredrik's face lit up.

"You mean it? That's... that's fantastic! Oh, that's great!" he said, grinning from ear to ear.

"You can take jumping lessons with it too, if you want!" I said, to tempt him further.

"Well, then it's settled. I'm in! Well, most likely anyway. Since we seem to like the same type of horse, I assume that I'll be fine with your new one too," he said, looking a lot happier than he did a few minutes ago.

"I'd like to... I'd be happy to help you find a good home for Penny," he then said.

"That's the least we can do for her!" I nodded, and together we gave her some energy feed and brushed her a little before taking her back to the pasture.

Fredrik biked home while I stayed for a while helping Linn bring in the horses for the evening. It was almost eight thirty, and I liked the fact that Linn let them stay outside for as long as possible in this nice weather.

"Would you take Nikita, please?" Linn asked nicely when we got to the bay mare's paddock. I nodded, and Linn went inside to fasten a lead rope to the halters of the other two ponies. They came willingly and followed her happily, knowing that there would be tasty hay and energy feed waiting for them inside. Nikita looked more hesitant.

"Sweet little Nikita – come!" I called. She looked uncertainly at me, as if she was considering whether or not she ought to go with me. Finally she decided to let me put the lead rope on her, since both of her buddies were on their way into the stable. She walked calmly next to me, glancing around curiously.

"You're actually pretty fond of life, aren't you?" I asked quietly. She snorted and threw a glance at me. "If it wasn't for that hopeless owner of yours, you probably wouldn't be so jumpy either..."

After we got into the stable, I led her to her stall and she stood still while I took the halter off of her, and then she walked over to the hay that Linn had just thrown into her tray and started eating. Her coat was still stiff and gray with hardened mud, and I noticed that her stall hadn't even been mucked out!

"She could sure use a cleanup, and her stall too," I commented, nodding toward Nikita. Linn nodded, and got a worried look on her face.

"That means that Martine hasn't been here today!" she said. At this stable, it happens rarely, if ever, that nobody is around to muck out and take care of a horse. Either the owner does it, or a horse groom, or an exercise rider. Mucking and grooming the privately owned horses is not Linn and Anette's responsibility though, and they're supposed to be told if the rider will be arriving after 8 pm. With regard to the stable horses, which are kept in a summer pasture, there's more freedom, since they're not affected by closing time at the stable.

"So she's been covered with this mud since yesterday afternoon! It's too bad that she has to stand here caked in mud for seventeen hours, but I simply don't have the time or energy to do volunteer mucking for no-show horse owners!" said Linn with an irritated expression on her face. I nodded in complete agreement.

"Would it be okay if I did it, do you think? I wouldn't mind," I said, surprising myself. Linn looked questioningly at me.

"I can't stand the idea of the poor thing standing here another night like that," I said, fully aware that I was making it sound a little worse than it was. It's not like the horse would die or anything.

"Hang on, I'll call her," said Linn, and went to get the

cordless stable phone which had the numbers of all the horse owners on it.

"Hi, it's Linn!" said Linn, surprisingly friendly, into the phone.

"Any particular reason why you didn't come to the stable today?" she then asked, still in a friendly tone. There was a short silence. Absentmindedly, I stroked Nikita over the muzzle every time she raised her head, which was quite frequently. Then Linn said, in a more short voice:

"In that case, do you mind if Julia cleans her up? She's all covered in hardened mud. And the stall really needs to be mucked out too." Linn listened for a few seconds, then she said goodbye and hung up with a headshake.

"She sounded completely distant, and said she didn't have time to come! But she said you could brush her if you want to, so you go ahead. It's really nice of you to do that, Julia! Bye now." Linn left quickly, and I saw her walk toward her house, which was near the jumping arena and the trail that leads into the woods.

I was filled with a childlike joy at getting to cuddle and brush Nikita. I got my cleaning tools and started working. She sniffed and watched me curiously while I worked, and didn't get the slightest bit upset, even though I was disturbing her in the middle of her evening meal. A full hour later, she looked like her beautiful, brown self again, her stall was clean and filled with fresh, soft straw and shavings, and I even got her a little extra hay. Then I gave her a big hug before I left, unlocked my bike, and headed home, wondering what my mom was going to say about me coming back closer to ten than to eight, as I had told her. Oh well, it was summer, after all!

That night I wrote the ad to sell Penny. I put a lot of thought and effort into the wording, because I wanted it to sound as serious and professional as possible. Then I sent a copy of the ad and a short message in an e-mail to Fredrik. For some reason it felt appropriate to do that. After all, he had ridden Penny for two years, and I thought he had a right to know as much as possible about the sale. I gave a deep sigh, resting my head in my hands, and both of my parents came over and read the ad over my shoulder, nodding slowly. Dad gave me a comforting pat on the back, and then they left me alone. After staring at the screen for a few seconds, I hit "Send," and with that, Penny was up for sale...

Next morning, it was still pretty hot outside, so I contemplated whether I should just take Penny for a leisurely walk. Then I remembered – Pia was supposed to be back today! She had been on vacation for four weeks, and I cheered up considerably at the thought of seeing her again. I called her, and she said she'd be at the stable in about an hour.

After eating a quick breakfast, I got on my bike and headed to the stable, enjoying another wonderful morning ride. On my way there, I met Linn, who was leading Proud Misty. He was already saddled up, so they were obviously going to ride. She smiled and said hi, and I smiled back. For a moment it looked as if she wanted to say something else, because she stopped briefly and hesitated. I looked at her, a little curious, but then she continued walking, as if she had changed her mind at the last minute. The gelding walked proudly next to her, and was practically bursting with energy. I watched him admiringly, and as I went into the stable I couldn't help wonder what it was Linn had wanted to say. I found out soon enough.

"Hi, little Nikita!" I cooed, walking over to her. As usual she came to the stall door and pressed her muzzle toward the bars. Then she greeted me with a low snort. I felt my insides get warm and fuzzy with joy, and gave her a light kiss on her little white collar. Suddenly I heard a strange noise, but the horse didn't seem to react to it. There was the noise again, and it sounded like it came from inside Nikita's stall! Slowly, I opened the stall door, and now I could tell what the sound was: sniffling! I was more surprised still when I saw that the person sitting there, wiping her tears, was none other than Martine!

Chapter 14

"Martine...? Is everything alright?" I asked, totally shocked to see her like this. Martine looked even more shocked to see me, and quickly started wiping away the tears and fixing her brown, ruffled hair. She glared at me, almost hatefully.

"What do you think? Would I be sitting here crying if everything was all right?" she shouted. Nikita jumped and took an anxious step toward me. Martine's outburst surprised me, but I chose to ignore her anger.

"No, of course not," I said. "Poor choice of words, that's all. Can I sit down?" Again, I was surprised at myself. Why would I want to sit down with the person I disliked more than any other? With somebody who treated horses as if they were things! Martine nodded briefly. I sat down in the straw, and for a while we just sat there opposite each other. For a split second I was tempted to give a sarcastic comment about it being a pleasure to clean up Nikita last night, but instead I tried to be as friendly as I could, asking calmly, "Do you want to tell me what's wrong?"

Martine hesitated. The hostile look in her eyes was gone. Now she only looked miserable and sad.

"Okay... I might as well tell it like it is," she finally said. I waited for her to continue. "I've been kicked out of the stable. I'm out of here – just like that! Linn told me just now, right before she went to get her stupid horse," she added. I raised my eyebrows, but let her finish.

"She said that the way I treat Nikita is 'totally unacceptable' and 'against the stable rules and regulations' (this last part she said with childish mockery), and the fact that I wasn't here yesterday didn't help either. So now I've been booted out of here," she finished with a heavy sigh.

I didn't know if I should feel more sorry for Martine, who sat there whimpering like a little kid who didn't get her way, or Nikita, who just had to go with her owner to a different stable where they may not care as much about the horses' well being. Of course, it's no fun being kicked out of a stable, but to be honest, it was rather well deserved, I thought...

"Oh, I'm sorry," I said, trying to sound sympathetic.

"Well, I'll finally be able to quit riding, though!" she suddenly exclaimed, and this surprised me more than anything! As I was still watching her in shock, she continued, with a strange look on her face. "Dad's the one who wants me to ride. When I started taking lessons at a riding school three years ago it was fun, or at least kind of fun. But after I got my own pony it all turned into a drag that just took way too much time and effort, not to mention the pressure for me to win at events and stuff... I hate it! What I want to do is play soccer. Why can't he understand that?" Suddenly she burst into tears again, and I sat down next to her and put a hand on her shoulder. I was totally unprepared for what Martine had just told me, so now I found myself seeing the situation in a new light.

"You know, I don't even think I'm particularly fond of animals! Of course I love Nikita, but... I don't understand her, and she probably doesn't understand me either. So one thing's for sure – I'm going to sell her. I'm sure she'd be better off with an owner who's gentle and patient. Somebody who loves horses, and likes to compete. Because she's really good, you know. She's only eight years old, but before I got her she'd won several prizes in Easy B and Easy A dressage, and she loves to jump. And she's totally sound too." Martine took a deep breath after this long string of words, and then she started speaking again. "Julia, I'd be willing to give you a good offer. I'm sure she's dropped in price since I got her, anyway," she added with a sad smile.

I looked at her in total bewilderment, so she looked straight at me with her brown, serious eyes. "You do want Nikita, don't you?"

Chapter 15

A good hour later, after our happy reunion, Pia and I sat in Penny's pasture together. It was great to see her again! I told her everything – from riding in Spain, getting home and having to make the difficult decision to sell Penny – right up to the last thing, that I had practically gotten a new horse already. Pia gave me a big hug.

"Are you telling me there won't be any more crazy, wild trail rides for us anymore?" she asked with an expression of childlike disappointment. I laughed as I shrugged my shoulders.

"Maybe later, when I've had Nikita for awhile and she's gotten used to me and feels more secure," I said. I got all warm and fuzzy inside as I thought that Nikita was possibly going to be mine!

"But tell me, did Martine just ask you out of the blue if you wanted Nikita?" asked Pia, wanting more details. I nodded and continued.

"At first I was in total shock, you know! But then I thought about it, and it suddenly occurred to me that Nikita is, in fact, exactly what I want and need! I've visited her several days in a row now, and she's so wonderful. And apparently she's also very talented, and..." I rambled.

Pia rolled her eyes at my new "passion," and pushed me teasingly. "Yes, Nikita is very cute," she said, "but have you even tried to ride her yet?"

"No, but I'm going to tonight!" I said, jubilant, because I was convinced that she'd be great.

"Martine went home a little while ago to talk to her dad and to bring the necessary papers, a sales contract and stuff, and I'm going home to talk to my parents. I don't expect them to have a problem with it, because they've already agreed to buy a new horse, and since I'll get Nikita at a pretty reasonable price, I... The only problem is that I haven't sold Penny yet! I hope we can afford to have two ponies boarded for a month or two," I said, suddenly stern. Pia looked at me.

"I'm sure it'll work out somehow," she said. "But right now, I'm going riding," she shouted, and then she walked over to Prisci. The two of them had just reunited a little while ago, and Penny and Prisci had been grazing near us as we talked.

"There now, sweetie," I mumbled to Penny as I put on her halter. "You'll finally get to ride with your best friend again!" Penny nodded her head and snorted loudly, and I laughed lovingly at her.

"Poor things, they'll be separated," said Pia suddenly as we led the ponies down to the stable. I instantly knew what she meant, and realized that I hadn't thought about that! When I sold Penny, she and Prisci, who had been

118

like two peas in a pod for almost a year and a half, would be split up and have to live separately!

"You're right! Ohhh, that'll be so hard on them," I said with a sigh. "I sure hope they both get a new horse to be with, so they can forget each other and get over it as quickly as possible." Pia nodded, but I detected an expression I couldn't quite interpret. I watched her as she led her darling pony, which had really put on weight over the summer. It occurred to me that Pia must be at least four inches shorter than me, and skinnier. *She'll probably be able to continue riding Prisci for a long time still,* I thought. Prisci was much wider than Penny, and Pia didn't have my long legs, so she probably wouldn't outgrow her anytime soon. *No fair!* I thought.

We saddled up the ponies (Pia laughed when she saw that she had to tighten the cinch a couple of notches further out than normal, because of Prisci's stomach), and started riding. Pia was tan after having been in France and Italy for so long, and we chatted away about our vacations. Even so, I noticed that Pia wasn't as lively as usual, and when I told her about my trail ride with Eline, she got very quiet at first.

"Did you really ride with that cranky old thing?" she finally asked, and I was taken aback at how irritated she sounded.

"Actually, she was very nice!" I said in Eline's defense. "And she really knows her stuff!" I added. Pia just shook her head, and then she patted her pony on its dappled, round behind.

"Guess we have some training to do, to get you back

119

in shape, darling," she said lovingly to her pony. "We'll start off slow, with some trotting, then put in some intervals of galloping, and increase the intensity little by little. We've got do some eventing this fall, you know!"

"Oh, yes, there's going to be an event here at the end of August, actually!" I said, happy to bring good news. Pia's face lit up.

"How fun! You'll sign up, won't you? What classes will it be? What kind of judging?"

"I'm not completely sure about the classes. Linn is going to put up the lists in the stable soon, I think, but there will at least be Easy C and Easy B and..."

"What?!" yelled Pia. "It's dressage?!" Pia almost spat the last word out. I looked at her with surprise as I nodded.

"Ugh, how boring!" she said, wrinkling her nose. "Come on, let's trot!"

It was after one o'clock when I rode my bike into the driveway at home, skidding on the gravel in front of our garage. I hurried into the house. Mom was busy vacuuming, but turned it off and sat down when I asked her to.

"Guess what? I've found the pony I want!" I blurted out. Then I explained to her all about Martine and Nikita in detail.

"Well, your dad will be home around five, so we can probably both go over there with you. Did you say you're meeting Martine at seven?" asked Mom with a little smile. I was so happy, and I gave her a bear hug, making her laugh out loud.

On our way to the stable, I told my mom and dad about Nikita, and I noticed that he and mom exchanged a smile every so often. We walked up through the avenue of trees, but I started running when I saw Nikita. She came to the fence to greet me! I gave her a piece of carrot and she let me scratch her forehead. Dad came over to us and let her sniff his hand.

"Well, you sure are a sweet and pretty girl," he said in a soft voice, and Nikita snorted contentedly. Just then Martine emerged from Stable B accompanied by a tall, stocky, and very serious-looking man, who I assumed was her dad. When I thought about it, I remembered seeing him several times before, whenever Martine was competing in riding events. Still serious, he greeted my parents and me, and while the three grownups were talking Martine asked me if I was ready to ride Nikita. Was I ever! We went into the tack room, where she got Nikita's things for me. With a look at the sharp Pelham bit, the noseband and the martingale, I knew I wasn't going to want to use any of it. I wasn't sure if I was being rude, but asked anyway. "Do you have another bit for her, by any chance? And I don't think I need the martingale." Martine looked surprised, but she seemed calmer than before, almost relieved in a way.

"Yes, I do," she said, and started looking around in the closet. "But I was told it's a good idea to use a sharp bit if the horse is difficult, so I did." She shrugged her shoulders, and I got the impression that she had never reflected on the fact that it would be very painful for the horse, especially when the rider is as hard-handed as she was. I pulled out the lower noseband from the bridle and put it in the grooming box, and after a while Martine stood up, holding a slightly dusty but perfectly good double-jointed bit. We took the tack with us outside and laid it over the tethering post before I went to get Nikita. She came willingly, but stopped and waved her ears uncertainly when she saw Martine by the tack. Martine looked a little sad, but walked away and joined our parents, who were standing by the dressage arena, talking. Nikita stood still and enjoyed the brushing. As for me, I was already feeling a growing fondness for her! I also noticed that she had a pretty stocky neck, something she probably developed from holding her head so tensed up in the air every time she was ridden.

"Don't worry, we'll get rid of it eventually," I promised, stroking her on the neck. "We'll also have to train your rear muscles. You don't have much strength in your hind legs right now becasue of the way you've been ridden."

She pulled away when I approached her with the bit, but I just laid the reins calmly over her neck, and when she realized that it wasn't the Pelham bit I was holding, she opened her mouth. When we were ready, I led her over to the arena where I tightened the girth. She tossed her head irritably and laid her ears back. But I knew that Martine had always tightened it fast and hard, often too tight, so I didn't blame her, and just ignored this behavior.

"Well, this is exciting!" yelled Mom when I mounted, and I nodded, feeling a tense knot in my stomach. What if it didn't go so well? What if Nikita really was as impossible as she looked when Martine rode her? What if she started bucking and trying to throw me off? *Quit it, Julia!* I told myself sternly. Besides, it was too late for regrets now...

Nikita stepped nervously but stood still while I adjusted the stirrups and the reins. Gently, I pressed the leg aids against her sides, and she took a few slow steps forward. I reminded myself that over the last year Nikita had been used to sharp spurs and poor riding, and so I tried not to have high expectations. She walked tensely, in an inefficient, stepping walk with her head up high, so I decided that the first thing we were going to do was to relax. I gave her loose reins on both hands as we walked around the arena several times. After a while, she lowered her head and stretched her neck. I could tell that she had relaxed a little, but as soon as I picked up the reins she shot her head up and got tense again. So I kept giving her loose reins, and picked them up several times to make her understand that she could continue to relax. Then I shortened the reins and started riding in a variety of directions. I was very focused, so when I looked up, I saw to my surprise that I had attracted a bigger audience. By now, Heidi, Michelle, Eline, and Camilla were all standing by the fence next to Martine, her dad and my parents. They were talking to each other, as they watched Nikita and me very intently.

We rode some serpentines and small eights, and after a few minutes Nikita started responding to the reins and positioned her hind legs more underneath. Her walking

gait gradually became more fluid, and when I finally started her in a trot, she was nicely bent with a little collection. She was great! I gave a gallop kick, and she rushed forward into a fast, unbalanced gallop. I took a deep seat and asked for a half parade, and at that, she suddenly put her hind legs underneath, bent her neck beautifully, and her gallop felt like a dream. She was as smooth as silk! I asked her to gallop, but after only one round she started breathing heavily and slipping out of her collection, so I slowed down to a walk and slackened the reins. Her hind legs, back and stomach were so weak that she couldn't walk with a collection for very long, but I felt excited and happy at the thought of working with her. I guess I had decided then and there that I had a new horse!

Chapter 16

The whole thing went surprisingly fast. Before I knew it, I was Nikita's new owner! I was overjoyed, and spent many hours at the stable every day. Martine didn't seem the slightest bit jealous because Nikita was walking so nicely for me. She just seemed relieved that I wanted her. We signed the papers in the evening on the same day that I first rode her. Both my parents and I signed, as well as Martine and her dad, of course. My parents also let a few hints slip to Martine's dad about the importance of letting young people do something they really like and have a talent for, instead of being pressured into activities they aren't interested in. And Martine hasn't shown up at the stable since that evening. The last I heard was that she's playing on a soccer team, and supposedly having a great time.

So everything turned out for the better! That is, except for one thing... Pia had been very distant toward me lately, especially after I bought Nikita, but I decided to talk to her about it as soon as possible.

"Pia!" I yelled, running up through the tree-lined driveway, from where I always left my bike. She stopped and looked at me with raised eyebrows.

"I can't stand having you be mad at me! Would you please tell me what's wrong?" I asked.

"All right then. It's just that... Well, it feels like you're growing up so fast, that you're growing away from me, kind of. You'll be competing in a totally different league than I will, you're really good at dressage, and we can't go on our usual wild trail rides any more. Prisci and I... well, we're kind of stuck in the same place... in a way," Pia blurted out.

I just looked at her for a moment. Then I gave her a big hug and started laughing out loud. She looked surprised, but smiled.

"You silly girl! How could I be growing away from you? I'm as young as ever! And even though we'll be competing in different classes, we'll still be going to the same events, where we'll cheer for each other and help each other. And you and Prisci are terrific at jumping! Don't forget how you two beat Penny and me in every single jumping event! You're certainly not stuck. And of course we'll ride together, and be as wild as ever! Nikita is actually a pretty tough little mare. Once her nerves settle down a little, and she learns to trust me, we'll be so wild and crazy, you'll be begging for mercy!" I finished, almost triumphantly.

Pia had broken into a fit of laughter while I was rambling on, and now she wiped away a tear of joy. I recognized the usual warm, teasing look on her face.

"Okay, Julia! Race you up the hill! On your horse!"